MUMMY

Also by Caroline B. Cooney:

MUMMY

CAROLINE B.
COONEY

ISBN 0-590-67450-1

Copyright © 2002 by Caroline B. Cooney.
All rights reserved. Published by Scholastic Inc.

12 11 10 9 8 7 6 5 4 3 2 1   2 3 4 5 6 7/0

Printed in the U.S.A.   01

SCHOLASTIC INC.
New York Toronto London Auckland Sydney
Mexico City New Delhi Hong Kong

ISBN 0-590-67450-1

12 11 10 9 8 7   0 1 2 3 4 5/0

Printed in the U.S.A.   01

First Scholastic printing, June 2000

MUMMY

One

Emlyn had a bad streak.

She was well aware of it and kept it contained. Others might yearn to be the hero and save the world or save the baby. Emlyn yearned to be a brilliant thief. Not your bloodthirsty type. Emlyn would never hurt anybody; never use a knife or gun.

But she was continually making mental notes: seeing a place to stash loot, a situation crying out for photographs or blackmail, or trust where there should be locks. She set these notes on the shelf in her mind where she stored her wrong plans. As the years went by, it became an entire library in her head. Wrong things to do, and how to do them.

If other girls were daydreaming about how to obtain a secret from a pharmaceutical research lab, or how to smuggle things on planes or falsify papers, they certainly never said so.

Once Emlyn read a list of favorite fantasies. It was in a slick and glossy woman's magazine, with pencil-thin models whose makeup and hair had a cruel geometry to make you shiver, or a wild lioness look to make you jealous. Between those covers, at least, fantasies revolved around beauty, sex, fame, power, and money.

Emlyn was more interested in ways to acquire money. Especially ways that might seem illegal to some. She loved the phrase "insider information." O! to be an insider who knew more and could pull it off.

She had no idea what she'd spend the money on. Who cared? Emlyn did not enjoy shopping and could never think of anything she needed. She just wanted to get away with things.

As time went by, she understood herself better. First, she wanted a great plan: a terrific, twisted scheme. Second, she wanted to make it work. Third, she wanted never to be caught.

Emlyn believed she could have all three of these. The main difficulty, as Emlyn saw it, would be the temptation after the theft to tell other people what you had accomplished. It was clear to Emlyn that your triumphs must be personal. You would do your wrong thing, and do it brilliantly, but then it must be kept inside you forever. You could not share it. With anybody. For any reason.

But of course Emlyn did nothing wrong, at any time or for any reason, because she was a good person, with good parents, attending a good school among mainly good people.

Instead, she did things like study hard and sing in chorus and work on her watercolors and learn Spanish and star in volleyball and get bruised in field hockey and take up crew. Emlyn loved rowing. She loved the river below her and the rhythm around her.

By the time Emlyn turned sixteen, she had done nothing wrong in her life, except an occasional fib. She had stolen nothing, except a pencil once or twice, and that was by mistake.

She began to feel that she could outgrow this desire to be deeply, successfully bad.

She was at an age now where boys and girls began to date with some intensity, and she had begun to consider boys with a certain hope and ache. She began to dress for them, posture for them, flirt with them.

But around the edges of her soul, and sometimes taking over her entire soul, so that nothing else mattered — not family, not boys, not clothes, not studies, not rowing — was a deep, thick yearning to do something — anything! — that you were never, never allowed to do. To do something so wrong that your essential self must go into hiding.

When she felt like this, Emlyn rowed.

She had a rowing machine for seasons when she could not go out on the river. She could pull on those pretend oars, pull herself into sweat and out of larceny. She took up running because there were very few days of the year when she could not run. The pounding, the demand, the gasping exhaustion of running took away the darkness inside her.

She took up reading, also, but not romance or suspense. She never bothered with adventure or fantasy. She read books that were supposed to tell you how to lead your life. How to Do such and such or How to Be a Better so-and-so. She read essays by famous Americans from Jefferson to Emerson. She read ancient philosophers. She was the only person she knew, religious or atheist, who had actually read the Bible.

The Bible was unexpected. Its stories made clear that from time immemorial, people not only *wanted* to do things wrong, they rushed right out and did them, over and over. If she ever zeroed in on her wrong thing, Emlyn would have company.

But fortunately, or unfortunately, Emlyn had lots of family, and she loved them. Her parents were happy with their own lives and work, as were her two brothers. Her uncles and their families lived in the same city, and they often gathered for picnics and dinners and day trips together. Emlyn was labeled as the calm, studious, athletic cousin.

It would destroy her family if they actually became acquainted with Emlyn's true self.

Philosophers, from Plato to Thoreau to her English teachers, spouted the belief that you should be yourself. "No matter what, be true to yourself!" they cried.

Emlyn's true self, however, was not a good one.

She had kept her true self a complete secret, but now, in the first half of her senior year of high school, Emlyn was finding it more and more difficult to refrain from Bad.

4

And so when Jack and Maris and Lovell and Donovan approached her with their scheme, she knew that she had never had an offer so wonderful. So perfect. So true to herself. So necessary and wrong and beautiful.

She would do it no matter what.

There was no question in Emlyn's mind.

But whether she would do it with Jack and Maris and Lovell and Donovan was another thing entirely.

"It's an interesting idea," she said, keeping her voice bored and her face bland, to imply that it was actually a foolish and unworthy idea.

Their faces fell. Emlyn's first triumph at Bad. She had acted, and they had believed her. Their idea no longer seemed so beautiful.

She now possessed the idea, and it was just as beautiful as they had thought. But she wanted it for herself. Casually, she said, "What made you think of me?"

This was important. Had they somehow seen within her soul? Seen that dark spot? Was she an X ray to them, and over the white bones on her negative was there a spray of badness, as clear as a tumor to a radiologist?

"Well," said Jack, "you never talk, Emlyn. You just do things, and ace them. You don't brag, or make excuses, or discuss."

Jack had grown astoundingly, probably six inches in six months. His flesh had not kept pace, and he was lean and bony and mismatched. Girls loved measuring their height against the thin tower that was Jack.

If he wanted to be hidden or anonymous, his

height would work against him. He was impossible to miss.

Jack said, "We figure nobody can keep a secret the way you can, Emlyn."

Jack's girlfriend, Maris, leaned forward. She was the lioness type, tawny and gold and powerful. Maris said, "You don't gossip, Emlyn. I have never heard you say a good word or a bad word about anybody."

Emlyn in fact loved gossip and stored all of it. But she did not contribute. She had to be careful. How could she be anything else, given her personality?

"Museums cannot be easy to steal from," said Emlyn. "Surely the city museum has up-to-date security and plenty of guards and alarms."

As a matter of fact, Emlyn knew that it did not. When others went on field trips to the museum for art class and wandered in boredom, filling in their sheet of questions about Impressionist painters, or when they went for history class and wandered around filling in their sheet about medieval armor, Emlyn filled in her sheet for storage in her mental library of Bad.

How to stay in the museum past closing.

How to fool the guards.

How to outwit the supposedly hidden cameras in the Sculpture Hall.

"So you don't think we can do it, huh?" said Donovan.

If Emlyn were going to fall for a boy, it might be Donovan. He was the kind of guy who just started and walked till he got there. He had no plan, he was not particularly smart, he created no strategies. He just saw the goal and started moving. Whether it was math or baseball, a science paper or car repair, Donovan had a relentless, sturdy approach.

He was the sort of person you would want with you in war or disaster.

Or crime.

Emlyn beat this thought down. Donovan, she knew, was a good person. In his case, it was not faked. It was one of the things that attracted her. Perhaps if she became close to him she would learn how to be like that, or at least to imitate goodness more easily.

She said, "Donovan, I'm surprised you want to be a party to this."

He nodded. "Me, too. Actually, I had plenty of other ideas, but Jack and Maris and Lovell didn't think much of them."

Emlyn respected the opinions of Jack and Maris. Therefore Donovan's ideas had been second-rate. But she said courteously, "What were they?"

"Well, last year's senior class managed to get two llamas up there," said Donovan, tickled by this memory, "and so I was thinking we could do a cow."

"Staying with animals," said Emlyn encouragingly.

"And the year before that, they got the chassis of an old Camaro up there, and I was thinking we could do the vice principal's Miata."

"Cars are nice," agreed Emlyn. She knew

7

where the vice principal kept her purse and car keys, and it would be the work of a minute to obtain these.

"Or," said Donovan, "I was thinking maybe the principal's desk. Put it on a hoist, you know, let it swing. Papers flying. Maybe hang the chair, too, and a filing cabinet."

"That has possibilities," said Emlyn.

"No, it doesn't," said Jack. "Every senior class has done either an animal or a car or something that belongs to the administration. I mean, *boring*. Our class has to do something really really really special." He gave a tight, little, excited-with-himself smile and opened a folder. Inside lay drawings and photographs. He removed a post-card and handed it to Emlyn. She could actually see his fingerprints on it. Emlyn held the post-card neatly between her two palms, leaving no prints.

She loved getting away even with that. She loved the image of the FBI finding this, trying to call it evidence, but never able to prove that Emlyn had held it.

Like most of her fantasies, it was ridiculous, and she knew it and laughed at herself — but only half laughed.

The postcard was from the museum gift shop. It was in color. Its background was a dark, gleaming room with stone and pillars. Resting on a granite base about three feet high was a heavy wooden slab about five feet long. A glass case like an aquarium was fastened to the wood.

Inside the case lay a mummy.

Emlyn knew the mummy well. Her parents were Friends of the Museum, and Emlyn had spent many rainy Sunday afternoons putting up with dull exhibits so that eventually she could stand next to the mummy and think about the three thousand years in which that mummy had stared at a ceiling.

The mummy was straight and slim, rounded where her arms were tucked, and running smoothly down to the triangle of her protruding feet. Her wrappings were intricately woven in basket-weave layers, and over the centuries had taken on a stained look, as if people had spilled tea over her. Partly covered by the wrappings was a face mask, painted on papier-mâché made of papyrus.

Beautiful sad dark eyes and the lovely soft mouth of a young girl looked up into eternity. The mummy wore an intricate necklace of blue paint and gold leaf, and the terrifying amulet on her forehead was a glittering, many-legged beetle.

The hieroglyphs on her wrappings identified her as Amaral-Re. Princess.

Emlyn handed the postcard back and shifted her book bag so that she would have something to cling to. She did not want Jack to see that she was trembling with excitement.

"So," said Jack, "our class has to pull off a really exceptional trick for Mischief Night. Therefore, I thought of the mummy."

"*I* thought of the mummy," said Maris sharply.

Jack and Maris gave each other tiny glares and then smiled stiffly.

Emlyn thought, They date, they hold hands in public, they buy each other presents. But they don't actually like each other.

Emlyn said, "I really can't imagine stealing a mummy."

She could imagine it perfectly. She was going to do it. But she didn't want these four in the way.

Donovan was too open, too practical. Jack and Maris were too vivid, too demanding of attention. She thought highly of them separately, but together they were busy sticking pins in one another and might not be reliable. Those three could never do anything quietly and in secret.

Lovell was an unknown. Lovell hadn't been in a class with Emlyn since second grade. That made Emlyn uncomfortable. She had not yet executed one of her schemes, but she knew it would be risky to work with a person she barely knew.

"But can't you just see it, Emlyn?" said Lovell, in a mysterious whisper. "The bell tower on the old high school, open to the wind and weather? The huge steel beam on which the bell once hung and from which students in the past have hung llamas and the chassis of a Chevy? And this year, hanging in the night? Swaying in the starry dark? A real, honest-to-God Egyptian mummy."

It had been lyrical and correct until Lovell said "honest-to-God." Whatever else stealing a mummy might be, it did not involve honesty with God. It did not involve honesty.

So Lovell was a girl who did not even listen to

10

herself. She did not actually know what she was saying, or why. And Emlyn was sure that in theft or embezzlement or larceny, you must be sure of what you are saying and why. "So how come you aren't doing it yourself, Lovell?" said Emlyn.

Lovell giggled. Her laugh was fluty and appealing, and she expected the others to join in. Jack and Maris did. Donovan did not.

Certainly Emlyn did not.

Lovell said, "I don't want to get caught. I mean, it's a joke thing, really, and you wouldn't — like, you know — get arrested or anything. Like, the museum people, once they understood it was just a high school thing, you know, traditional and all, and Mischief Night before Halloween — they'd be cool. But still, they might not be. And I — like — I don't need that on my record."

Emlyn smiled sweetly all around, letting her smile rest a little longer on Jack, the ringleader. "But you think *I* would *like* to be caught?" said Emlyn.

"No, no, no," said Jack. "We work on it together, as a team. If something does trip us up and we get found with the mummy, Emlyn, you're the kind of person who can talk us out of it. You led that debate, remember? Nobody could touch you. You practically won even when nobody in the entire auditorium agreed with you. I know it was an assignment and you didn't care about your side and you didn't agree, either, but you were so convincing."

She remembered the debate vividly. The teacher had chosen a real-life local issue: Should

11

a toxic waste dump (which the city must have) be placed on the old elementary school grounds near the river?

Naturally, nobody thought it should.

Emlyn had been assigned to take the positive, and she loved her assignment. She slept with it and cozied up to it, acting as if she planned to manage the toxic waste herself. She didn't win the debate, but she got an A and a standing ovation.

Emlyn had been downcast. She didn't care about applause or grades. She cared about winning. Well, it turned out she had won after all. She had won Jack and Maris. They thought she could talk her way out of anything. She would start by talking her way out of this.

She said, imitating Lovell, "Really, I don't know what to say. Like, I'd love to hang with you guys, and I'd love to, like, be involved if you're going to use one of Donovan's great ideas, like the principal's desk and chair, I mean I love that, and his papers flying in the wind? That's, like, excellent. But I mean, stealing?" She gave a laughing shrug and spread her hands. "I mean, I think, you know — jail and all. And my parents and all. But good luck. I hope you make it."

She had, of course, timed this speech, because third lunch was twenty-one minutes long, and Emlyn always knew exactly how much time she had left, and she needed the bell to ring so she could make a graceful exit, with no more explanations or exchanges.

The bell rang exactly when she expected it to, and everybody laughed in a silly way except

Donovan, who didn't understand random laughter. Then they separated.

If Emlyn had not been a very controlled person, she might have begun yelling and walking on the wall. Mainly boys wall-walked, but if there was nobody watching, Emlyn sometimes raced down the hall and managed a footprint or two on the wall. But she paced evenly to her next class, said a courteous hello to the teacher (she was one of only a handful of kids who bothered), and sat neatly at her desk.

Emlyn got high grades in participation, even when she never participated, because she kept her eyes glued to the teacher. It was one of her favorite deceptions. It was not wrong, and yet in a tiny way, it was. She never ducked her head, never hid in her book, never slid behind her own hair — and never said a single word or asked a single question.

The two classes following lunch required immense self-discipline on Emlyn's part. She did not permit herself to think of the museum.

When school finally ended, Emlyn's heart shot into the air. She felt like a Frisbee, thrown across green grass in a fine, clean swoop.

It was the most wonderful idea in the world, even if Maris or Jack had thought of it.

Stealing a mummy.

13

Two

The Egyptian Room was half-lit by long, narrow windows whose glass had strange yellow panes. On the walls was painted plaster taken from a tomb, on which flat, sideways-facing Egyptians in white linen skirts were fishing and tending cattle. There were pieces of statues, including two feet with toes so long they looked like fingers that any moment might start knitting a sweater.

There was a Rosetta stone — pretend, of course, because the real one was in the British Museum in London.

The inside wall was a piece of a temple: columns and some steps, a thing as big as a classroom. Small children could squeeze behind the columns and ambush their friends and make them scream.

But in the center of this room was the only

object that really mattered to small visitors.

The mummy.

Even the littlest children understood that this was a dead person. The only dead person they had ever seen. And yet they could not actually see this one, either, for she was wound in hundreds of yards of narrow linen strips. How terrifying was her solitary confinement. The children who were there at the same time as Emlyn were awestruck and afraid.

The mummy was a princess. Her hand had once touched the cheek of a pharoah. Her fingers had once held a glass. Caught the clasp of a necklace. Played with a cat.

She was an object now. Property. A thing.

How brave you are, thought Emlyn, to lie exposed. Staring at ceilings for all time. A princess who expected to lie in a pyramid beneath the sands of Egypt. Wrenched from her darkness. Imprisoned in a dusty room in a second-rate museum in an ordinary city in America.

And now, I will rob your tomb again.

Emlyn actually changed temperature thinking about it. A great heat of excitement flushed through her core.

A guard drifted into the Egyptian Room. He barely saw the small children and the parents, but his eyes landed on Emlyn and studied her. Teenagers were not often here of their own free will. Teenagers, when asked about the museum, would say, "I went there when I was little."

Nobody in high school came here *now*.

And teenagers never went anywhere alone. They were always among friends; they moved in

15

packs, or at least in pairs. Emlyn was visible because she was alone.

The guard moved into another room. Emlyn loved his vague unease. He was not suspicious of her, he was just aware.

If you knew . . . thought Emlyn, and she was deeply, wonderfully happy.

She studied the mummy again, reading the old, tired cards that lay beneath the glass next to the mummy.

In the Egyptian Room, the cards themselves were historic; probably written eighty or a hundred years ago. In square, spidery writing, the ink slowly losing its color, some ancient curator told everything he knew.

The mummy's genealogy was unclear. Who were her parents? To what pharoah was she related? In what era had she been born?

It was known that in 1898, an American traveler purchased Amaral-Re in a street bazaar in Cairo. This, said the card, was common. Mummies were everywhere, under the sand, tucked in tombs, sold on streets.

In England, the wealthy liked to have mummy parties, and the mummy would be hacked open after dinner, presumably with much laughter and delight, and the amulets found inside the wrappings would be distributed as party favors, and the broken bones and linen would be tossed in the garbage.

Amaral-Re, however, had been kept on a pedestal on the balcony of the American's mansion. When he died, he gave both the mansion and the possessions to start a museum. The

16

museum's collection had long ago outgrown the mansion, which was now merely a quaint office wing attached to the real museum.

Amaral-Re was no longer on her balcony. The donor's will required that the mummy be displayed so that the children of the city might forever find the fascination that he had found in her mysterious eternity.

A second card explained that because the mummy needed her body in the afterlife, she had been dried out so she would last. Her lungs and stomach had gone into separate jars. She'd been cleaned with palm wine, and then for seventy days covered with a salt called natron, until she was a dry, stiff husk.

Amaral-Re had been only four feet eleven inches tall. There was a painted stick standing next to the mummy, so living children could measure themselves and compare.

Suppose, thought Emlyn, that in life Amaral weighed one hundred pounds. If a body is seventy percent water, and if the embalmers dried all water out of her, there would be thirty pounds left.

Thirty pounds was the weight of the scull Emlyn rowed and carried easily from the boathouse. So carrying her won't be a problem, thought Emlyn. Only hiding her.

Emlyn's fingers actually itched from the desire to touch the mummy, and she had to rub her hands together, as if to soothe a rash.

After Amaral's body was dried out, the card continued, she had been washed with hot resin, an oil from trees, to keep her soft. (Emlyn imagined this as maple syrup.) Then came hundreds of yards of bandages. With every wrap, the linen was brushed with more sticky resin, which glued the layers together and made them stiffen. Her linen was high quality; she was no common housewife wrapped in old, torn clothes.

The guard was drifting her way again. Emlyn did not want him to remember her, so she moved ahead of him, slowly taking herself into Birds. Just why Birds was adjacent to Egypt, Emlyn did not know. Birds was a hideous room. Most little children would not even go into it, and those who were dragged in began to sob right away.

Three hundred thirty-one different stuffed birds. How evil they were: glass eyes glittering, beaks apart. Even friendly birds, like robins, were stiff and hostile on their twigs. What would they do if they knew she was going to steal their neighbor?

Would they sing and fly with sweet abandon, thrilled that at least somebody was going to be set free? Or would they attack with sharp beaks and vicious claws?

Stop it! she said to herself. They are stuffed animals, and that mummy is a stuffed person. They have no emotion. They have no meaning.

The guard continued his circuit on into the next room, so Emlyn went back to Egypt. She stared at a dusty diorama opposite the mummy. Along its painted Nile were lotus flowers and papyrus. Slaves and rowers and geese. Baskets and urns and priests.

Emlyn fell into the diorama.

She could hear the oars dipping into the Nile

as pharaoh's royal barge slid by. She could hear the beating of stork wings as they left the shelter of the papyrus. She felt the leather strap of sandals between her own toes and the soft dark fur of the preening cat against her leg. Dry, baking heat rose from the distant desert and laid itself against her cheek. Her hair was heavy, bound with a gold band and knotted at the bottom, like the fringe on a scarf.

"Would you mind moving over a bit," said a parent politely, "so my children can see, too?"

Emlyn stumbled away.

Amaral-Re lay as calmly and silently as she had for three thousand years.

Three millennia ago, you ran and laughed and sang, thought Emlyn. And then, for thirty centuries — one hundred generations — you've been dead.

You were dead before the Crusaders, before the Pilgrims, before the wars of Napoleon, before the computer. You were dead before Mohammed, before Christ, before Buddha. You have known death for so long.

And in that long, incredible space of time, who else has owned you?

I will own you next.

Emlyn touched the case that covered her mummy. It was not glass. In spite of what the ancient card said, it was Plexiglas or some other kind of plastic. Therefore it weighed very little. Lifting a glass case five feet long, two feet high, and two feet across would be difficult for one person. Lifting plastic was not.

Perhaps the real purpose of the lid was to keep

19

Amaral-Re safe from the fingers of children, and their peanut butter, and their gum. To keep bacteria away, in case her dry bones had any points of weakness that might still be invaded by microscopic creatures and destroyed.

So the enclosure was not to prevent theft. It was to prevent touch.

We won't only be touching her, thought Emlyn, feeling a cold, sick shudder, like the first winter wind. We'll be lifting, flinging, tying with plastic cord. Hanging her from a tower, exposed to American weather — she who needs dry desert air.

But there was no climate control in the museum. Her container did not protect her from humidity. So even the museum did not care about that.

The guard would soon be back. Emlyn did not want him to see her a third time. She found the great stairs that went down to the first floor and wandered through museum rooms that meant nothing to her.

Unless, of course, she decided to invade them at night, and without permission.

Three

Dinosaurs was the first room a museum visitor entered after paying the fee and getting a colored tag. In the center of an enormous space stood a brontosaurus on a bed of stones, separated from the public by a low brick wall and a lot of signs that said PLEASE DO NOT TOUCH.

Touching, however, was the goal of every child.

The immense brontosaurus was supported by curved steel beams strong enough for a road bridge. Anybody could see that it was strong enough for a kid to climb. All across the Dinosaur Room came high-pitched arguments from small children who wanted to climb brontosaurus's spine, up to the ceiling.

Even now, Emlyn wanted to. But she sat quietly on a wide, backless bench and considered other things.

When I take the mummy, I'll come as a visitor. I'll just stay after closing. That should be easy enough. The crucial part is leaving. I'll be leaving with something everybody can recognize. Every one of these four-year-olds could yell, "That lady's got a mummy!"

It was not possible for Emlyn to think of an ordinary circumstance in which a girl might be carrying a mummy. Therefore, she must disguise the mummy as something else or leave by night when she could not be seen.

The first seemed impossible. Dress the mummy in something from The Gap and pretend she was taking a sick friend out to the car? People would notice that the friend was actually dead, and had been for three thousand years. Plus, Amaral-Re did not have separated arms and legs; she was a cylinder with a head bump and a feet bump.

Emlyn would have to stay here alone in the night and sneak out into the dark city with a mummy in her arms.

After a minute of eyeing brontosaurus, the older children began yelling, "But where is tyrannosaurus rex?"

"The museum doesn't have one," explained the parents. "Let's look at the camarasaurus instead. Or the edaphosaurus!"

Nobody cared about them. Nobody ever would. No tyrannosaurus rex? Sadly, the children concluded that this was a loser museum.

Only fifty steps and five minutes into the museum and visitors under eight were exhausted.

Toddlers wept from frustration, and first graders begged for snacks.

Way high up on the walls were wonderful painted murals of dinosaurs eating plants and one another. Nobody thought of looking up.

Emlyn studied the corners of the enormous room for cameras and sensors. She did not believe there were any. The hall with the valuable paintings and the hall with the sculpture, yes; the cameras were obvious, hanging in the ceiling corners. If there were cameras here, they were hidden, and Emlyn did not believe that this museum could afford state-of-the-art surveillance systems. Here, the museum used a living guard. After all, this was the room most likely to sustain damage. Sure enough, when Emlyn lowered her gaze, she found a guard studying her.

She was the thing in the room that was wrong.

Nobody looked up. Five-year-olds looked across. Twelve-year-olds looked at one another. Sixteen-year-olds didn't come.

The dinosaur crowd was shorter and younger than Emlyn, with less vocabulary. She was not a mother, nor a grandmother, nor a baby-sitter. It was the guard's job to notice somebody out of place.

She turned her attention once more to the brontosaurus and thought, I will outwit him. I will outwit all of them. I will get in. I will get out. I will have a mummy.

Children abandoning Dinosaurs rushed through Impressionist Paintings without slowing down or waiting for their parents. They spilled into the Sculpture Hall, a boring room with statues set into alcoves and standing on squares of granite and basically getting in the way of your race to the café. Emlyn let herself be swept along with a scout troop on a field trip. Tapes and short films were everywhere. After kids poked buttons to make them play, they ran on. The tapes played to empty rooms.

Suddenly Emlyn saw what she had never seen before, even in her most larcenous moments: Each gallery was separated by heavy iron grilles that swung out like café shutters. They were not Gothic decoration. At night they would be closed and locked.

A little boy tried to climb one. The guard didn't seem to mind and neither did his mother. He got about halfway up, was unable to dislodge it, and could not make it swing. He tried to fit behind it, but he could not squish under or through.

If I get stuck in a room overnight, thought Emlyn, I'll really be stuck. I might be able to find a corner and stay here alone in the dark, but I won't be able to change rooms.

This was sobering. What if she got the mummy in her arms but could not leave?

She walked slowly to the Great Hall, the only part of the old mansion still used by visitors. It rose in a golden dome, sparkling with tiny windows.

When Emlyn's mother was a girl, the museum had consisted only of the old stone mansion, a horrid, frightening place with a cageful of monkeys trapped on the stair landing and parrots screaming from an enclosure on a balcony. Looming out of dark rooms were colossal Greek statues, and gathering dust in corners were collections of nothing in particular. The mummy and this wonderful room were the only traces of the old museum.

Why would you have a room like this in your own house? A state legislature might want a room like this, but ordinary people? On the other hand, not much was ordinary about a man who went to Cairo and bought a mummy at the corner store.

Not much is ordinary about me, either, thought Emlyn, and she had to lower her eyes to veil her excitement.

Among columns and arched openings were two old-fashioned wooden doors. Stenciled in gold on one was SECURITY. Stenciled on the other was MUSEUM OFFICIALS ONLY. NOT FOR PUBLIC USE.

That, then, was the door that brought you into the old rooms of the mansion, once dining room, parlor, and butler's pantry, now offices. Emlyn stared at it with longing, but she turned around and left the museum. The only exit was next to the only entrance. You could not come and go without passing a metal detector and a guard.

Emlyn went outside and down huge, wide granite steps that also gave the museum a state capitol look. She crossed the street to walk around the museum on the far side.

The north wall was a flat, doorless, windowless expanse. This was the theater where they showed movies with subtitles. She was not going to shinny up ropes with or without a mummy in her arms, so this side was useless.

The east side had a high but roofless wall, with one regular door and one extremely large garage door. Neither had an outside handle. Could this be a parking and delivery area? Emlyn retreated half a block and sat on the curb, eating a bagel from a vendor's cart. Fifteen minutes later a car pulled up, facing the garage door. The driver tapped his visor, which must have held an automatic door opener, because the huge door slowly opened upward and the car entered.

Emlyn caught a glimpse of a garbage Dumpster, a few parked cars, a van with the museum logo, and a high cement walkway, the right height for a truck to back up to. So there was at least one exit from the museum into the utility parking.

The garage door folded back down, and the east wall was solid and silent again. The two door outlines facing her had to be emergency exits as well, and therefore they'd never be locked. Opening them probably set off an alarm, but you would be out in one step, across the street in ten, and vanishing into the city before anybody could react to the alarm.

You would, however, be holding a mummy.

This might alarm other people on the sidewalk.

Emlyn walked to the south, mansion side. The old stone house had many windows and doors. They still had their big round brass handles in the shape of lions' manes, but they also wore signs that said NOT AN ENTRANCE.

Inside high windows and behind the curve of elaborate drapes, she could see people at desks.

She walked back to the public entrance side and stared at the huge steps. The whole idea seemed ludicrous. When she'd been near the mummy, Emlyn had believed. Now she did not. The whole thing could not happen.

It was this detached calm that made it possible for Emlyn to take her first real step toward Bad.

She reentered, showing the little metal button on her shirt collar that proved she was a legitimate visitor. She went directly to the Great Hall. She walked up to the door that said MUSEUM OFFICIALS ONLY. NOT FOR PUBLIC USE. She opened it and walked in.

Four

The secretary could not have been nicer. She was so pleased that the high school newspaper hoped to carry an article about the new direction in which Dr. Brisband was taking the museum.

Emlyn deduced that this woman was not the mother of teenagers. Any real parent would know that there were no teenagers in this city or any other city who cared what direction a museum went in. If there was such a thing as a school newspaper (and in Emlyn's school there was not), they would know better than to waste good column space on museums.

But the secretary picked up her phone and said, "Dr. Brisband, I know how very very very busy your schedule is at the moment, but could you possibly fit in a high school reporter? Or perhaps you and she could determine a suitable hour during which you might give an interview at a later date?"

Emlyn was glad she had her purse with her and that in her purse was a small notebook and a sharp pencil. She could look quite reporterish. She wondered how long it would take to arrive inconspicuously at the subject of security systems.

Through the open door of the secretary's office she saw a small sign with an arrow. FREIGHT ELEVATOR. Well. That would bypass the iron grilles, would it not?

The secretary hung up. "He's on the phone, but he expects to be off momentarily. I'm so pleased it's going to work out. Sometimes he simply cannot squeeze another person into his very very very busy schedule."

"What a help you must be to him," said Emlyn.

The secretary admired Emilyn's outfit and wished that other teenage girls would dress so nicely. Emlyn chatted about Western High and what a great place it was. Emlyn herself went to Eastern.

"He wants you to wait in the Trustees' Room," said the secretary, and from the middle drawer on the righthand side of her desk she removed a large key ring. Emlyn thought there must be fifteen keys hanging from the brass circle.

"I can never remember which is the master," confided the secretary, "so I have it marked with a little blue tape."

Emlyn agreed that keys were such a problem. She herself was always mixing up her front- and

29

backdoor keys. What sympathy she had for the secretary, with so many many keys to juggle.

The secretary led Emlyn down the hall and opened up a room that must once have been the mansion's library. It held a stunning and immense table surrounded by twelve chairs of the sort used by the writers of the Constitution. Over its grand fireplace hung a painting that most people never saw, and Emlyn had a feeling it was the finest painting in the collection, reserved for the finest people.

This was where potential donors were fawned over. Where reporters were tucked so that they would be impressed.

"He'll be with you shortly," said the secretary, "and if by any chance he isn't, I'll be back from my cigarette break in ten minutes, and I will rescue you." She beamed at Emlyn, and Emlyn beamed back.

The secretary was in desperate need of nicotine. She darted into her office, tossed her key ring back into the drawer, yanked open another to pull out her pocketbook, and from the pocketbook took a pack of cigarettes and a lighter. She tapped on another door, and it was opened by an equally desperate smoker.

Doors to both offices were left open, and the two women rushed to the exit.

Emlyn looked around the Trustees' Room. Row upon row of old books with beautiful bindings covered the shelves, as entombed in here as a mummy in a pyramid.

Shockingly, a section of the paneled wall suddenly tilted inward.

30

It was a hidden door! So the mansion builder — the mummy buyer — the museum donor — had also been a builder of secret compartments. I wish I had known him, thought Emlyn, and a corner of her imagination drafted plans for the house she would build one day, with hidden doors just like that.

Sitting on a swivel chair at an enormous desk was the man who must be Dr. Brisband. He had opened the panel from his side. Cupping one hand over the phone and smiling as if she had made his day, as if talking to teen reporters was a highlight in the life of a museum director, he said softly, "I'm going to be another ten minutes. I'm so sorry. Please look at any of the books, and I will fit you in just as soon as I can."

She tried to look embarrassed. "I'll be right back," she mouthed, pointing toward the hall. Let him think she was going to the ladies' room.

He gave her a sort of salute and continued his discussion on the phone, and the secret door closed slowly and silently.

Emlyn stepped into the hall, crossed into the secretary's office, and slipped her right hand into the thin pocket of her linen jacket. The secretary hadn't even fully closed the key drawer. Using the pocket as a glove, Emlyn scooped up the key ring. The thin silk lining snagged on the sharp edge, but she got her fingernail beneath the double brass loop and removed the key with the blue tape and slid it into her pocket. She replaced the key ring and left the drawer as it was.

The key was too small to be weighty, and yet it carried the burden of all her years of wanting to do something Bad. For the very first time, Emlyn really was taking something that was not hers.

She had stolen.

So far it was a tiny crime. But it was the key, literally, to a larger one.

This is how it works, she thought. Opportunity comes and you seize it.

She felt incredibly alert. Her eyes seemed to take in a hundred times more detail, and her ears memorized sound and speech.

At the end of the hall, the exit door was propped open for fresh air. Standing in it, backs to her, were the two smokers, their hair and their smoke shimmering in the October breeze.

Emlyn went back out into the Great Hall and walked swiftly once more through all the rooms of the museum. For the second time, she went outside. When she passed the guard at the metal detector, her body broke into a sweat.

But no buzzer sounded. No eye met hers. She trotted down the steps. She was low on time. She knew her city well, but the location of hardware stores was not something she had previously considered.

Copy shop, shoe store, coffee stand.

Newsstand, dress shop, real estate agency.

Antiques emporium, flower shop, carpet store, grocery.

Please, she said in her heart. Please.

She felt as if she had been hiking for blocks, had spent hours, and still there was no sign of —

There it was. A hardware store.

Thank you, she thought.

And wondered, To whom am I saying please

and thank you? God? The fates? City planners?

"Hi," she said cheerfully. This was no time to be worrying about God or the fates. "May I please have a copy of this key?"

"Sure."

It took twenty seconds to cut, grind, and smooth. With a pleasant smile, the clerk handed her two keys. One dull and used; the other gleaming, having never entered a lock.

She thanked him and paid. She put the shiny key in her pants pocket and polished the old key thoroughly with the lining of her jacket. Before she reached the museum for the third time, she took off the tiny colored metal tab that every visitor was given at the door. She tied her jacket sleeves around her waist and yanked out her blouse, so that she was a person in a green shirt instead of a person in a pale linen jacket. Her hair was long and obedient, so she tied it in a knot at the back of her head instead of letting it fall on her shoulders.

A different volunteer accepted her Friends' card and handed her another metal tab. Emlyn hiked back to the door marked MUSEUM OFFICIALS ONLY, hoping the cigarette break had been long and satisfying. On the way, she tucked her shirt back in and let her hair down. She was shrugging back into her jacket as she opened MUSEUM OFFICIALS ONLY, and inside the office hall was crammed with people.

Oh, no, thought Emlyn. They discovered the missing key? They phoned Western High and found out it has no newspaper?

But whoever these people were — curators?

volunteers? janitors? security? — they coagulated in little clumps and then dissolved out various doors, revealing the secretary coming back from her break. She was surprised to see Emlyn in the hall.

"There's always a line at the ladies' room," said Emlyn. "Isn't it annoying?"

"Oh, truly." The secretary rolled her eyes. She walked on by and into another office, so Emlyn slipped into hers and put the old key back on the ring. It took seconds. She had not known how fast Bad things went by. Then she ducked back into the Trustees' Room.

There was no sign of Dr. Brisband, and his marvelous door was shut. She could not even see where it had been, it fit so beautifully into the molding.

Emlyn removed her notebook from her purse and wrote a little note:

I'm so sorry you did not have time for the interview after all.
I will call and perhaps you can fit me into another time slot.

Thank you.

It did not say which school. It included no phone number. She had not used her own name. He might retain a vague memory of her for a day or two, and he might vaguely wonder when she was going to call, but most certainly he would not call any of the city's public high schools, or Catholic schools, or private schools, or its one boarding school in the hope of arranging such an interview himself. In a few days neither he nor the secretary would remember her.

For the last time she left the museum, and this time, standing at the official exit, was the guard who had watched her while she watched Amaral-Re.

"Enjoy the Egyptian Room?" he said.

"I love it there," she said. "I'm hoping to be an archaeologist one day and run my own dig in Egypt." This was completely untrue.

He grinned. "Don't we all? I never look at the mummy without wishing I could find the next Tutankhamen."

"Do you ever feel, when you're standing among those ancient artifacts, that you've fallen back into ancient Egypt?" said Emlyn. "Does anything exciting ever happen to you when you're here alone at night, in the dark, with the mummy?"

He laughed. "A museum is never exciting," he said. "Especially at night. Nothing happens. No statues come alive and no mummies walk."

Emlyn laughed with him. But he was incorrect. One mummy was going to walk.

Five

The following day, Emlyn walked down the hall on the second floor of her high school. She was neither messy nor stylish. Her khaki pants and white shirt were pressed, and her navy cotton pullover sweater was just baggy enough. Her hair was loosely pulled back in a ponytail. She wore no makeup. She wore no jewelry.

All around her were girls trying desperately to be noticed. Some wore extravagantly strange clothing. A few had tattoos. Some had colored their hair weird shades or shaved it. Some (invariably girls with enough money to shop in the best places) were amazingly shabby.

Emlyn rejoiced at the ordinary way in which she blended in.

She had hit upon the word *caper*. Prank would be the act of hanging the mummy in the school bell tower. But caper would be the act of removing the mummy from the museum.

Jack, Maris, Lovell, and Donovan would have the prank.

She, Emlyn, would have the caper.

It was not going to be "stealing." Stealing was much too serious a word. It implied police and a criminal record. This was simply the annual high school Halloween event. People would laugh, even Dr. Brisband.

The moment Amaral-Re was hung in the bell tower of the old high school, the school would notify the museum, which would zip over in its little van to rescue her. At that moment, the museum would know why the mummy was taken. But they would not know who had taken it.

Emlyn was determined that nobody would know she was part of it.

Emlyn never wanted to be noticed. She would not pierce her tongue or cheek with jewelry, and she wouldn't pierce her reputation with a mummy theft, either.

For Jack and Maris and Lovell and Donovan, this was a one-time thing. They'd probably love to be identified with such a grand trick. But Emlyn intended this to be the beginning. She could not be identified with it.

How, though, could she take the mummy without Jack and Maris and Lovell and Donovan knowing?

She would have to give them the mummy in the end, because she did not want to do the prank part, only the caper part. But suppose they could not be trusted to stay silent? Suppose they told on her?

Suppose Emlyn called it a caper, but other people called it stealing? What was a mummy worth? Tens of thousands of dollars? Hundreds of thousands? You surely could not buy a mummy on the streets of Cairo anymore. Egypt would never permit you to take an ancient object out of the country now. So here in America, the mummy was beyond price. And if taking it was a crime, what would the price of the crime be?

If she took it on — and the key, light in her pocket, seemed evidence that she was taking it on — she took on the risk of being caught. The risk was incredibly exciting.

But risk meant the possibility of losing. If she lost — if she got caught — what would her family do?

There was a comic aspect to this, but Emlyn's parents would not laugh. She was their firstborn, their pride and joy. She was their easy child, the one about whom they could always boast, and did. Her brothers were almost primitive in comparison. Having them around was like living with short barbarian warriors.

And if the barbarian with the primitive impulse turned out to be Emlyn, what would it do to her parents?

A heavy hand suddenly rested across both her shoulders and the back of her neck. It tugged her hair and wrapped partly around her throat. It felt like a hairy snake.

It was Jack.

There was no reason why he should not be

38

friendly with her in public. He was not giving away the details of any conspiracy. But there was something triumphant in his touch; something possessive and hateful. Stop it, she said to herself. He's perfectly ordinary, it's my imagination that's out of line. "Jack," she said, instead of hello.

"Emlyn," he said. "We need to talk." He was trying not to laugh. It wasn't working. His mouth and his cheeks were losing the battle, and his laugh was coming out.

"About what?" said Emlyn.

He stopped walking, which stopped Emlyn also. He was not gripping her; it was more of a block. "Emlyn. Maris and I went to the museum yesterday, too." His voice was very soft. "We saw you there. We followed you. We followed you into the museum, and we followed you out of the museum. We didn't go back in with you the second time. Or the third time. We just sat on one of the benches in the little corner park and laughed."

They had seen her? Followed her? Counted the number of times she had come and gone?

No. Impossible. Far from being hidden, a perfect blend, an invisible, ordinary citizen, she had been an easy mark. How could she not have looked behind her? How could she not have scanned the crowds for people she knew?

Jack and Maris? Oh, she could imagine them giggling to each other. Pointing. Sneaking after her. Jumping back behind pillars if she started to turn.

She was no clever caper organizer. She was a bumbling idiot, trotting from one hall to another,

39

taking notes, gaping at guards. She had hidden nothing from anybody.

The guard from the Egyptian Room had probably memorized her face. Her features were pinned up in his memory as a potential worry, the kind of person who threw acid on fine paintings and had to be institutionalized for life.

Do not cry, she ordered herself. Be an actress. Just because I failed and Jack and Maris are laughing at me doesn't mean I will break down in the hall. "I don't see how it can be done," she said with a shrug.

"Maris lifted the mummy," said Jack. "We wanted to see if alarms went off. None did."

"Lifted the mummy?" repeated Emlyn, stunned.

"Yup. That lid just sort of peels upward. It wasn't easy, but Maris and I got it up a few inches and she stuck her hand in. The mummy isn't attached to anything. It's just lying there. Maris got two fingers under it."

"But what about the guard? And weren't there people around? The museum was packed because it was free day."

"We were drowning in little kids and parents. As soon as the guard moved through Birds, Maris and I just did it. One father yelled at us, and two mothers said, 'Stop that!' and the guard came back and Maris said to him, 'The case moved. How come it isn't fastened down?'"

Emlyn would never have done anything in front of people. But after all, what was the guard to do? Shoot Maris? All he could do was glare and tell her not to touch again.

"The guard said he was reporting this incident, but he didn't take our names, so I'm not worried. *You* were the one skulking in the corners, Emlyn. We just sashayed out and learned what we needed to know."

She felt as if she had undressed in a room whose shades she had thought closed and whose door she thought sealed; and here, two people had been standing there observing her naked.

"What class do you have now?" he asked briskly. "Can you skip it?"

"World Literature. I can't skip it." Emlyn never cut. She liked class. She liked the position of her own desk and the feel of her pencils between her fingers. She liked taking notes and seeing her intelligent arrangement of the teacher's discussion on her own page. She liked when they showed a film and she could sit in the dark and dream. She liked analyzing the personalities of her classmates and the way they talked and fidgeted and learned, or failed to learn.

But seniors were allowed to cut a certain number of classes per semester, no excuse necessary, if they were on honor roll. Emlyn was on high honors.

They had reached her World Lit class. Jack released her from the weight of his arm and walked on toward the stairs. He said without looking back, "Maris is cutting, too, but Donovan and Lovell can't. We'll fill you in on what we found out."

The humiliation was complete.

She could be a good little student and walk into World Lit.

Or she could tag along and find out what the competent people had learned that she had not.

Maris said, "You were so funny, Emlyn."

Emlyn tried to have no expression.

They were standing in the doorway to the music room. No class or rehearsal was going on. All music students felt free to gather here at any time. If somebody walked in, she and Maris and Jack could reach for their band instruments as if about to practice. But Emlyn wasn't in band this year. She couldn't fit it into her schedule, and the band director was angry with her because he was short on clarinets. She felt like an impostor in the band room door.

I was supposed to be the one who could be an impostor anywhere in anything, she thought, and I can't even do it in the music room.

"You were so cute, Emlyn, all wide-eyed and intent," said Maris. "Right near you was this four-year-old. He'd never been to the museum before, and he walked around the whole time with his little mouth hanging open and his eyes gaping. You looked just like that."

Emlyn did not know if she could survive being compared to a funny-looking four-year-old. "So there's no alarm attached to the mummy?" she said.

"Or anything else in the Egyptian Room," said Maris. "Those two glass cases that are basically tables? And they have jewelry in them? The signs says DO NOT LEAN ON THE CASE; ALARM WILL SOUND. Well, I leaned pretty hard, and no alarm sounded."

42

"The iron grilles are the problem," said Jack. "I don't know why I never saw them before. But they're definitely closed every night, because I asked. So what I can't figure out is how to get from one room to another. It doesn't matter how much we want the mummy if we can't get to it."

Emlyn felt a tiny bit better. She had written down (wide-eyed and intent as a four-year-old) the location of every grille. In fact, you could go from the freight elevator hall into the Bird Room, and there was no grille between the Bird Room and the Egyptian Room. You could get to the freight elevator hall from the offices in the mansion. Furthermore, from the Great Hall you could climb the huge old stone steps of the mansion, turn left through Mammals, and get to Egypt that way. No grilles. Of course, you couldn't get into the Great Hall to start with because of grilles — unless you came from MUSEUM OFFICIALS ONLY.

"Who did you ask about the grilles?" said Emlyn.

"The guard. After Maris shoved the mummy around."

"I didn't shove it," said Maris. "I barely even touched it."

What had it felt like? Was the linen rough or soft? Could you feel the resin, poured on and dried three thousand years ago? Was the mummy completely stiff? Like plaster? Or soft like a bedroll? But Emlyn felt too awful to ask.

"Anyway, the guard followed us," said Jack. "It was a kick. I never had anybody suspect me of doing something bad before."

43

"What would you have done if an alarm had gone off?" Emlyn asked Maris.

Maris shrugged. "Nothing. I'd have said, 'Oops, bumped into it, didn't I?' "

Maris had no fear, because Maris did not consider any of this wrong. You aren't afraid of using the stairs or drinking from the water fountain. So why would you be afraid of touching a mummy? Just because it was in a museum behind Plexiglas and had guards?

So why am I full of fear? thought Emlyn.

"Aw, Em. You just took it way too seriously," said Jack. "It's a joke, and it'll work or it won't."

Maris put in, "Donovan says another group of seniors wants to hang a pair of kayaks up there, stuffed with dummies of the vice principal and the principal as rowers."

"That's not funny," said Jack scornfully. "That's not even difficult. Kayaks don't weigh a thing."

"Neither do mummies," pointed out Maris.

"Yeah, but the mummy is so cool. It'll look so weird, swaying up there in the wind. We want lots of publicity for our class prank. A mummy is definitely the way to go. We get the mummy up there and call the TV station."

Amaral-Re. Princess.

Hanging on a cord, TV stations mocking her, students pointing and hooting, her dignity destroyed.

"Listen, Emlyn," said Maris. "We've made our plans. We've decided to meet tomorrow after practice. I'm in the play, and rehearsal ends around four thirty. Lovell has a soccer game, but it's home, she'll be done by five. Jack has soccer practice, he'll be done at quarter of five, and Donovan's out of work usually at six, but he's going to leave at five. We have to figure out a strategy. Now. What about you?"

The other four equaled "we."

Emlyn was "what about you?"

It might mean simply that Emlyn had not committed herself and the others had. But it might mean Emilyn would remain an outsider. If they or she were caught, the four who were "we" would stick together, and the one who was "what about you?" would be left to hang. As it were.

Jack ticked his fingers to make a list. "We have to figure out how to get into the museum. How to get the mummy out. Where to keep it till we hang it. How to get it into the high school and up into the bell tower."

Is Amaral-Re *it* or *her?* thought Emlyn. If the mummy is an *it,* then it's nothing but dried-up old history held together with bandages. But if Amaral-Re is *her,* then she is a girl, a beautiful girl whose family loved her enough to try to give her eternity.

"There are magic spells written on her linens," said Emlyn.

Maris shouted with laughter. "Emlyn, of all people! I would never have suspected you of worrying about ancient curses! I thought you were the most sophisticated of us, and here you're the most babyish."

They had stung her so many times now she felt as if she had walked into a wasps' nest. Pretty soon she would go into respiratory failure. "You guys are way ahead of me," she said. Her voice shook. She pretended to clear her throat, as if she were coming down with something.

Jack patted her kindly.

Maris looked amused. "Tomorrow, then, Emlyn?" Maris had not asked whether Emlyn was busy or when she would wrap up her sport or activity or job. "Under the two maples if the weather's good," said Maris crisply, "McDonald's if it's not."

Theirs was a city school, every inch of ground used for playing fields. There were few corners of free grass and only two trees. The maples were glorious, especially now that it was October. There might be other kids sitting beneath them, watching a practice or talking, but probably not. It was getting cold for sitting on the ground. The maples were a good choice.

McDonald's, however, a half block away, had been constructed with a second floor, a much-frequented high school hangout. Dozens of kids would see them together and listen in. If the weather was bad . . . well, she would deal with that tomorrow. She nodded.

Jack and Maris walked away, leaving Emlyn standing alone in the music room doorway. She felt like a walking exhibit of pride smashed.

And then she remembered.

She was the one with the master key.

Six

Emlyn's parents liked to know where she was but had long ago stopped checking. On a weeknight, Emlyn was expected home by ten and must let her parents know her destination. On a weekend, she could be out till one A.M. as long as her parents had a phone number and knew who was driving.

But they did not check.

After all, she was a high school senior and she had never let them down. And they had the boys to worry about.

Emlyn lived in an apartment building roughly halfway between her high school and the museum. The eight-story building was about fifty years old, and Emlyn and her family lived on the seventh floor. Emlyn and her brothers routinely ran up and down the seven flights instead of using the elevator, because the family was very fitness oriented.

Although there were parts of the city where school buses were used, Emlyn lived in an area where everybody walked. She rode in buses when she had an away game, and she did occasionally use city buses, but since she always felt the need for more exercise, she tended to walk or jog. Her own sports were crew, field hockey, volleyball, track, and swimming. She also had marching band, debate, and high school academic bowl. It was not possible to do all these every year. And this — her senior year — she had broken her wrist. The cast was off, but forget rowing or volleyball. Forget hockey sticks.

It was wrenching to be a nonparticipant. There was only so much pride you could feel in handing around water bottles. More than once, Emlyn had claimed a physical therapy appointment and extricated herself from a practice in which she could not join.

How incredible that she had been upset about a college application that would imply she could not play on a varsity level — but she was considering being criminal on a varsity level.

Emlyn tried to arrange her thoughts, but her mind was flying about like pieces of shrapnel. It had been years — middle school, probably — since she had felt such relief to have a school day end. She found her coach, who just nodded when she said she didn't feel well enough to sit on the bench, and then she left school and headed for the city library.

If Maris and Jack and Lovell and Donovan

had decided on tomorrow for a strategy meeting, Emlyn had precious little time to gather more facts.

The reference desks were so busy that nobody on the staff paid attention to anybody not lined up and pleading for help.

She would check out no books. The computer system saved checkout information. Emlyn did not want to be on record as having taken every mummy book just prior to the theft of the city's only mummy.

In the children's room, she found four excellent, highly illustrated books about mummies and one, unexpectedly, about the Metropolitan Museum of Art in New York.

It turned out that mummies had always been snatched. The concept of a mummy prank was not new. In Shakespeare's time, people ground up mummies and used them for medicine. Emlyn imagined being in bed with the plague or tuberculosis and having the doctor say, "Here, tincture of mummy."

It just went to show that people had always been sick and twisted; it hadn't started with Emlyn's generation.

It was Napoleon who set off the mummy craze. When he invaded Egypt in 1798, his staff sent back to France such exciting drawings that everybody in Europe must have rushed to Egypt to bring home a souvenir mummy.

Travelers to Egypt could buy mummies in the bazaar as easily as people bought sunglasses today. There were thousands of mummies because for hundreds of years the Egyptians, and later on Greeks and Romans who lived in Egypt, practiced mummification.

X rays showed who had been murdered (Tutankhamen) and who had had arthritis (Rameses).

Dental studies proved that Egyptians ground their flour for bread with sand, and wrecked their teeth, and lived in pain.

Emlyn felt the plump part of her palm beneath her thumb. Once a girl named Amaral, breathing the scent of the Nile, writing on papyrus, laughing among lotus blossoms — had also been happily planning her tomb and looking forward to death, when she could dry out like an apple core in the sun.

And then, of course, the big treat — lying forever, staring at the ceiling of her pyramid.

Ancient Egyptians.

You could show up at that Egyptian Room every rainy Saturday for your whole childhood and not be any closer to understanding what these people had been thinking of.

Emlyn was shocked to find that she had spent the entire afternoon leafing through children's mummy books.

She went to the pay phones on the lower level of the library where the little coffee shop and the magazine room were. She said hi to several high school friends. What if they knew what she was planning? Would they find her despicable? Or just a good ole classmate setting up a good ole class prank?

She phoned the museum, which had recorded messages from which you could exit to more detailed explanations. It would certainly be a kick in the teeth if plans were made for a day on which they couldn't get in to start with. Emlyn listened to every sentence of every choice.

And that was a good thing, because the Friends of the Museum were having a meeting that very night. Emlyn glanced at her clothing. She did look like a person who might show up for a Friends' meeting: tailored and academic.

Her parents were members, but it was just for the get-in-free card; she could not recall that they ever actually attended anything, and they wouldn't tonight, because her brothers' school had its open house. Her parents would be rushing from room to room, trying to meet every science, math, language arts, history, music, phys ed teacher, and administrator. They would be saying to each other, Isn't it wonderful that our daughter is a good girl and we never have to worry about her?

When Emlyn called home, her younger brother answered, which was nice. *He* certainly never cared where his sister was, and all she had to say was, "Tell Mom and Dad I'll be home by ten."

He said, "Sure," and that was that.

Next she hit the Internet, and as was often the case she was drowned in too much material. "Egypt" produced five hundred sites; "mummy" more than fifty. And because absolutely everything could be counted on to turn up on the Net, there was a site dealing with museum theft. Another site for Classical Antiquities Theft. Even a discussion of "movable cultural property."

Well, if she took Amaral, she would know where to look for insider updates.

Skipping dinner gave Emlyn exactly enough time before the Friends' meeting to go back to the children's room and glance at *The Children's Guide to the Metropolitan Museum of Art.*

Two sentences destroyed everything.

"As soon as the museum closes in the evening, cleaners get to work with mops and brooms and buffing machines. The cleaning goes on all night."

Emlyn had never dreamed that the museum would not be empty and silent at night. She had pictured hiding out in the ladies' room until all staff and visitors were gone. But that was the first place a cleaning crew would go. They would go everywhere. And they'd have every light on, to see the dust by.

Her museum was probably not a tenth the size of New York City's famous museum. Certainly nobody had ever bothered to write a book about it. But cleaning was cleaning.

She stopped off at a pizza counter and had a single slice of cheese pizza.

Would Dr. Brisband want some floor polisher whining during a Friends' meeting? Surely he would not want an important Friend in need of a bathroom to have to wait till the floor dried. Perhaps tonight there would be no cleaning crew.

I can take the mummy tonight, thought Emlyn.

There were about seventy-five people at the meeting, which was seventy more than Emlyn would have expected to show up. She saw no guards. They must be around but keeping a low profile. You did not want potential donors to feel they were not trusted.

She wondered if Dr. Brisband would recognize her. She doubted it. On the other hand, people who loved publicity and people who gathered donors (and Dr. Brisband must be both) had to be excellent at remembering names and faces.

Well, he had never known her name, but he might know her face.

With a sinking heart, Emlyn realized that she had given a name to the secretary. Regrettably, she did not remember the fake name she had given.

Wonderful, thought Emlyn. Brilliant strategist cannot even recall name.

She distracted herself by estimating the age of the other people at the meeting. She was the youngest by fifty or sixty years. The rest of the Friends looked as though they never remembered their names, either.

Should she pretend to be the same Girl Reporter she had been during her last pass through the museum? She had her notebook. She would have to be sure nobody saw the pages mapping grille locations.

Harris Brisband looked wonderful. Tall and elegantly slim, in a starched pale yellow shirt and a charcoal jacket woven through with an occasional red thread. His bow tie was bright and jaunty. He was definitely in love with his microphone. Emlyn could always tell when a person was crazy about the sound of his own voice.

"We are not a small, unknown city," said Dr.

Brisband, "and we should not have a small, unknown museum. We, tonight — you and I — are setting a new goal and heading in a new direction. We in this city must rise to the same rank as Cleveland's great art museum or Baltimore's!"

Emlyn did not think it sounded particularly exciting to be Cleveland or Baltimore.

"Our museum must cry out!" said Dr. Brisband, taut with excitement. The excitement looked real to Emlyn. Dr. Brisband was proud of this building, and all that was within it, and all that was to come. He was the kind of speaker who made eye contact with every person in his audience, drawing them into his arms and heart, and hoping also to draw their checkbooks.

Emlyn never looked away from a teacher's gaze, but she looked straight into her lap and pretended to be taking notes for her article about the museum when Dr. Brisband turned toward her.

"Our museum must tell the world: We have great art! We have magnificent sculpture! We have history and beauty and truth!"

Oh, that'll bring high school students by the carload, thought Emlyn.

She gazed up at the ceiling of the Great Hall, where the gold glinted back and the tiny windows were shiny from the night sky. The folding chairs were delightful old things: wooden slats and leather seats, and each seat back had a neat little leather pillow, like a dentist's chair, so you could rest your neck as you gritted your teeth. Emlyn rested her neck.

"Very few of the artifacts we possess are on display," said Harris Brisband. "We have so many things in storage. It's a crime. Boxes and crates of fine artifacts, none of which you have ever seen. Or ever will, unless we raise the money to increase our staff and expand our exhibit potential." He paused, and when he spoke again his voice had changed dramatically. "However, no matter how much money we require, we must honor the will and the intent of the founder of this museum. We must never be unworthy of his trust."

Emlyn slid into a coma.

What was she going to do with this mummy after she took it?

Suppose she got out of here, mummy in hand. Then what? The mummy was large and stiff. Emlyn lived in an apartment building where dozens of tenants used the same front door. They would notice her. At any hour of the day or night, the doorman would definitely notice her. That was his job. He was good at it. And she did not have a cellar or an attic. Apartments never had extra closets hanging around waiting to hold something large. And the mummy would have to be held for a while. Senior prank day was always Mischief Night, just before Halloween, *two weeks off*. If she figured out how to get the mummy tonight, she'd have a lot of other problems along with the mummy.

Dr. Brisband suggested that they move down the hall to Impressionist Paintings, where he had a new acquisition for them to gaze upon and there were refreshments.

Everybody was happy to hear the word *refreshments*. It didn't matter how cultural an event was. Whether you were a toddler or a grandparent, you hoped there would be food.

Emlyn stuck her notebook back into her purse. She knelt as if to tie a shoelace. Many rows of folding wooden chairs were between her and the exiting Friends. In moments, Emlyn was alone in the Great Hall. How long would refreshments hold out? Twenty minutes? An hour?

There are no iron grilles between me and the Egyptian Room, thought Emlyn. What if I go there right now? Right up those huge stairs.

She was shaking slightly. It was odd to see her hands quiver, as if she were older than the very old Friends with their silver hair and age-spotted skin.

If I go up there, she thought, first I have to lift the Plexiglas case. Do I trust Maris's version that it can be lifted easily? But say I get it off. I rest it against the wall. There is the mummy, waiting. I lift the mummy.

She was amazed by the depth of her desire to take the mummy and her terror of actually attempting it. She felt as if she herself were hanging in the bell tower, swinging like a pendulum from one choice to another.

She was trembling in places she had not known you could tremble. It wasn't visible. There was no quiver extending from her ankles to her fingers. But the tremor of excitement and dread was racing through every vein and artery.

She could do it now. It was literally within reach.

The wide stairs were rough stone, with bands of shining metal crossing each tread, and the banisters were also stone, carved and fluted for eager fingers to grip.

Go, she said to herself. Go.

The columns and shadows of the Great Hall overlapped and slid. If a guard was nearby, he was hiding like a little kid behind a pillar. Emlyn doubted that that was the behavior or the size of guards. Once more, Emlyn opened the MUSEUM OFFICIALS ONLY door to the offices. Lights were on, but nobody seemed to be there. When she closed the door behind her, it clicked loudly.

If anybody catches you, you're looking for a bathroom, she told herself.

She skipped the secretary's office, the Trustees' Room, and Dr. Brisband's office. Sure enough, the first unknown door she opened was the staff bathroom. It locked from the inside. She might need a door like that.

There was one more unknown door. Emlyn listened hard and heard nothing. The depth of the silence was heavy and complete. She opened the door fast, before she could panic. The room was empty. Just more desks, computer screens, and stuff. She found it hard to believe a museum needed all this.

At the back of the room was an original door from mansion days. Huge, heavy, and impressive, a door requiring a servant's strong arm so that a lady in a fine gown could pass through it. Emlyn required only a way out. Now she had one.

She went back to the arrow labeled FREIGHT ELEVATOR.

Around a corner was a final door that took Emlyn out of the mansion and into the museum, through a large utility hall with vinyl floors and an acoustical tile ceiling. There was the freight elevator. Buttons on the wall said UP and DOWN.

Her thoughts splintered and fell, like broken glass. Every thought had a sharp edge and the ability to cut.

She could take the mummy, carry it into the freight elevator, slip out that side door, and be free in the streets.

And then what? Bring the mummy home? On a bus? In a taxi? Her brothers would be awake, assuming the other passengers on the bus decided it was not their business if she was carrying a mummy. Her parents would ask about her day. "What is that?" they would say, although they would certainly be able to guess.

Okay, so that wouldn't work. Could she leave the mummy in the office? Put the mummy into some closet? Come back for it?

As soon as they found the mummy gone, a search would be launched. They might not think of searching office closets, but security would be tightened and locks changed. Emlyn would not get in a second time. Her key would no longer allow her to remove the mummy she had stashed. Nor could she again pretend to be Girl Reporter.

No, on the night she came for the mummy, she had to leave with the mummy.

Tonight would not work. There were too many details for which she had not planned. And no doubt more problems that she would think of when she pondered this. She must have these

58

solved in her mind so she wouldn't face them under pressure.

She could, however, explore the cellar. Find out what was down there and where the exits led and whether —

"What are you doing here?"

Emlyn turned slowly.

It was a guard.

Not one she recognized. Not the one with whom she had chatted at the exit yesterday.

"I'm so glad to see you," said Emlyn. "I'm actually shaking." She held out her hand for him to see. "I was using the bathroom in the offices, and I've taken the wrong door out. It's really scary here at night. I'm here with my grandmother, and she's always the one who gets lost, but now I'm the one who's lost. She's probably worried. You'll get me back to the Friends, won't you?"

She smiled anxiously, and it seemed that Jack and Maris were correct.

She could get away with things.

Seven

Of course, everybody but Emlyn was late for the meeting. Neither play rehearsal nor soccer practice was ever over when it was over. Things had to be put away; people had to shower and blow-dry their hair; arguments had to be settled and snacks exchanged.

Finally, closer to six than five, they were gathered by the two maples. One was scarlet, the other gold, making Emlyn remember the Brownie song she used to sing: "Make new friends, but keep the old; one is silver and the other gold."

These were not friends, and not one of them was silver or gold. What they were about to do was tarnished, and Emlyn knew it.

Lovell and Jack were still damp from their showers and very tired. Maris, because the drama department lacked showers, was sweaty and irritable. Donovan was just Donovan.

Lovell flung herself down on the grass, and one by one the rest joined her. Since they no longer had to see the stage or the ball, the girls did not bother to tie back their hair but let it fall, and their bodies drooped as loosely as their hair. The boys let go of their strength and fell back against the cooling grass.

How pretty we look, thought Emlyn. An art class should come and draw us in pastels or fling us onto watercolor paper.

"Okay," said Jack. "First. How do we get the mummy out? We can't just walk in there and some of us distract the guards while others of us pick the mummy up and run out the front door."

"Maybe we could," said Maris thoughtfully. "Lovell and Emlyn and I would each subdue a guard, while Jack and Donovan hoist the mummy onto their shoulders and run toward the exit like football players with a long, thin, flat football."

Lovell laughed.

Donovan said, "I still say a cow would be better."

"Donovan, stop your noise," said Maris. How attractive Maris was, in a bony way; her features would be visible from the back row of any theater, and in fact everything about her was theatrical — the way she flung words around, and gestures around, and even affection. She *was* drama. "We've settled on the mummy, Donovan. Emlyn's in with us. Emlyn and Jack and I crept around the museum the other day taking notes."

Emlyn certainly preferred this version.

"If the mummy bent at the waist and the knees," said Donovan, "we could use one of the museum's wheelchairs. While you were distracting the guards, I'd wrap the mummy in blankets and go down the elevator and we'd be home free. But it's stiff." He grinned. "That's the point, I guess. A mummy is a stiff."

They all smiled, but Emlyn a little less. She was pretty sure Donovan had thought of that yesterday and been waiting for the moment to wedge it into the conversation.

Donovan was equal parts ugly and handsome, put together in a sloppy, pleased-with-himself way. He was slouchy, as if he had extra bones he had to drag around and stick in corners. He was not a leader. He didn't join, he just left school and went to his job. Was he poor? Impossible, with those clothes. Or perhaps that's why he worked. To get clothes, a car, things.

"We could bag it," said Maris.

"You're kidding!" Jack was upset. "Maris, you want to give up?"

"No, no, no." She gave him a kiss. "Bags. A big black plastic trash bag to drop the mummy into and pretend to be taking something to the Dumpster."

Perhaps Emlyn was just envious, but the kiss did not seem to hold affection. It was more of a silencer. There was something casual between Jack and Maris that Emlyn didn't think would exist if they were truly fond of each other.

"No, because then we'd have to go disguised as janitors," said Jack. "You're making it harder, not easier."

"Somebody has to go into the museum in the afternoon as a regular visitor," said Lovell, "stay hidden until the museum closes, open a door for the rest of us, and we'll all go in and take the mummy except whoever will be driving the get-away car."

Lovell was an aggressive athlete. Powerful, quick and afraid of nothing. She had longer hair than Emlyn's, beautiful hair, but seemed unaware of it, the way a horse was unaware of its mane. She just lived under it.

"You've forgotten the grilles that will keep us separated from the Egyptian Room," said Donovan, "not to mention the guard who will come running."

Emlyn did not trust any of them. They were taking this as casually as Jack and Maris took each other. This was not a minor thing. It was not dangerous the way rappelling an ice cliff would be, but it was fraught with danger. Caught, as a group, having planned a theft from a city institution, stealing an important, valuable thing — yes, admit it, stealing — not a caper, not a prank — well, there was the possibility of police, fingerprints, a night in jail, court. A record, because they were over sixteen. Nothing they did now could be minor, because they themselves were not minors.

Only Emlyn had a shiver of apprehension. The others could have been talking about removing a subscription card from a magazine.

"Who would have thought this would be so difficult?" said Lovell. "Here we have this great idea and no way to get started on it."

63

It was time for Emlyn to say that she had a key. But she did not.

Anyway, she told herself, I'm not sure what I have a key to. Maybe it isn't a master key. If it unlocks only the Trustees' Room and Dr. Brisband's office, I can't even get to those two rooms from the Great Hall, because it won't open the MUSEUM OFFICIALS ONLY door. After the Friends' meeting, the door was just unlocked. I've never tested my key, I never even thought of it. What's the matter with me? I should have tried it out.

"Let's come back to that," said Emlyn. I'm not trustworthy, either, she thought, or I'd tell them about the key. I would never do this on a team. On a team you don't whine about your own little problems or your own little angles. You work together. So either I don't think we're a team, or I refuse to be a team. Either way, in a team sport, you can't win unless you all have the same game plan. So we're going to lose, unless we turn into a team. If we lose this game, the first stop is jail.

"Let's say we do get the mummy out," said Emlyn. "Then we have to put the mummy somewhere. We don't want to hang the mummy till the day before Halloween. So where do we store her? Where is there a place that's dry and dark and hidden and can't be found and has room for a five-foot stiff?"

"None of those details matter," said Maris impatiently.

"Think about it, Maris," said Lovell. "You're coming out of the museum with the alarm bells ringing, you're got a mummy on your shoulder, and it's two in the morning. Are you going to walk home with it? Are you going to have it sit at the breakfast table with you for the next two weeks? Are you going to shove it into your locker at school and hope nobody sees?"

"So take it the day before Halloween, and go straight to the high school."

"The school will also be locked at two in the morning," said Jack.

"So one of us will wait inside the high school to let you in. You guys are making this way too hard," said Maris.

"Maybe it *is* way too hard," said Donovan. "There's the getaway car, for example. If we lived in the suburbs we'd have our own cars, but nobody keeps two cars in the city. So we have to use our parents' car, and how are we going to do that all night long some school night? Or a weekend, either? And if we lived in the suburbs, we'd have attics and cellars and garages, and we'd just sling the mummy into a corner, but we don't. We have apartments without room for a bicycle. I have to keep mine chained in the hall. I sure don't have mummy space."

Lovell whipped out her calendar. "We can't take it the day before Halloween." She set her calendar on the grass, and everybody leaned forward to stare at the little square dates. "October thirtieth this year is a Thursday, and Jack and I have away games. Maris, you'll be in dress rehearsals. We can probably hang the mummy that night, but it already has to be in our hands. For me, the only time that's good is the Sunday before, and that means a week to hang onto it before we hang it."

"Pyramids look good, don't they?" said Emlyn. "Where else can a mummy rest, and not be found, and not get wet, or nibbled on by mice, or stepped on by passing joggers?"

Donovan was laughing. "Pyramids don't have maintenance problems, either."

"Cut it out," said Maris. "Come on. We have to think of something."

"A cow," said Donovan.

"It would seem to me," said Maris, "that a cow would also pose problems. It's heavy, it's fat, it doesn't want to be strapped to a hoist and lifted three stories into the air, and it would probably refuse to take the stairs, and its owner certainly wouldn't lend it to you. Stealing a cow is probably more wrong than stealing a mummy, when you think about it. Which one is alive?"

"And what if the cow stops being alive at some point?" said Lovell. "Then you'd have cow murder on your hands."

Lovell and Maris fell on top of each other, laughing.

"I don't think we're serious about this," said Jack. "We're kidding ourselves. Somebody else is going to have to pull off the good senior prank, because we're just a bunch of — "

"*Grave robbers,*" breathed Maris.

Emlyn, her back cold on the cold earth, cheeks damp with green grass, fell away from them into a dark, closed tunnel, where oil lamps sputtered and drafts of dead air wound around Egyptian ankles. She wore a linen robe and carried a chisel, and her heart was full of greed. She was savagely chipping and hacking a hole through

66

stone, wedging herself into a black room filled with the dead, filled with their bodies and the pieces of their bodies, lined with jars of liver and lung.

But the dead meant nothing to her or to any other grave robber.

The living did not care about eternity.

They wanted treasure.

Emlyn rolled over, climbing out of the king's tomb into which her mind had fallen. This had happened before. A little time slip, so intense, so detailed, with scent and dust and heat. She knew it was just the strength of her own daydreams, but she felt close to Amaral-Re for those seconds.

Emlyn stared up at indigo-blue sky. Tutankhamen had chosen that very deep blue for the color in his tomb, a blue so vivid it felt as if it could last forever and yet couldn't exist at all.

And I, thought Emlyn, what do I want? *I want to do this.* I know it's wrong. I should be disgusted with all of us. But I'm not.

I want to do this.

A theft is when you keep what doesn't belong to you.

So this is *not* a theft.

We will *not* keep the mummy.

She will *not* be damaged.

She'll just have publicity and a lot of admiring stares, and she's used to that.

A wisp of cloud shivered above her, a fragment of purity and white on that blue plate of sky. Very softly, she said to her team, "Here's how we'll do it."

Eight

Without letting them unfold from their package positions, Emlyn took two very large black plastic trash bags, the heavy kind for yard cleanup. She taped these around her left forearm with masking tape, which would be easy to remove. Then she put on a long-sleeved white cotton oxford shirt and wrapped several feet of masking tape around the right sleeve. Next she put on a charcoal-gray wool pullover sweater.

The plastic crinkled when she moved but didn't slow her down much. It was a lot easier than the cast had been.

She wore black twill pants, slightly baggy and very comfortable. In one pocket was her master key; in the other, a small but powerful flashlight in which she had just invested. Over this she wore a gray wool blazer of her mother's. In an inside pocket of the blazer was her very small cell phone.

She was not sure why she had decided to bring it. If she expected to have to call a lawyer, she should call off the idea instead. But a phone comforted Emlyn. She did not intend to use the basement of the museum. But if something happened and she had to hide in the dark — well, the dark was better when you could summon a voice.

She put her Friends' card into an outside blazer pocket along with a few dollars and some change. She tucked a pair of disposable plastic gloves in the other pocket and a pair of thin black knit gloves on top of them. She checked herself in the mirror for bulges. She looked ordinary.

It was Sunday afternoon. Monday was a teachers' workday, so there was no school. Her parents were going out for dinner with two other couples. Afterward, they had concert tickets. They would not be in till very late. Her brothers were staying overnight with friends. Emlyn herself was supposedly staying overnight with Lovell.

She had had trouble looking at her parents all weekend. She felt in need of a veil, a covering. She knew they were not scrutinizing her. They felt comfy around her; she was their good girl. If her eyes were down on her plate, it was because she was hungry, not because she was keeping secrets.

Her brothers were unable to keep secrets. They shouted out instantly when they did anything, whether it was good, bad, or meaningless.

Emlyn had lost track. Good, bad, and meaningless had come together in this senior prank, sloshed together like a painting she could not understand. She was a high-speed train, racing toward a new and shiny station — or a wreck.

Sunday afternoon passed slowly. It was like waiting to be put into a game. You sat on the bench feeling sick and scared, needing action but fearing failure. The minute you were in, the sick feeling went away. You were fighting; it was good.

Jack picked her up down the block from her apartment building.

He had borrowed his parents' van. It was huge and must be a real pain in city parking. But inside — what a great vehicle. Swivel seats, a bar, a little TV-VCR. Its windows were dark glass, so nobody could see in. Someone had brought a cooler full of soft drinks, and a grocery bag was bulging with treats, two kinds of chips sticking out the top. Nobody had much to say.

Jack drove to the museum, coming up the side street that faced the mansion. The other big, old houses once built in this neighborhood had been torn down a half century ago, and apartment buildings six or eight stories high had taken their place. There was not nearly enough parking for the residents. Street parking was difficult to find. Early in the afternoon, Donovan, who after much pleading and fibbing had managed to borrow his father's car for a short time, had circled the block over and over till a space opened up.

When Jack and the girls arrived in the van, Donovan pulled out, and Jack slid neatly into the space Donovan had been holding for them.

Emlyn could not parallel park. She could not imagine parallel parking a van as huge as this, where you could use only side mirrors. "Good work," she said to Jack.

"The work is all yours, Em. Good luck." He had food, drinks, his car phone, and some homework. He would be lying down on the carpeted floor of the van, invisible to the world, waiting for Emlyn and a mummy.

Donovan would take his dad's car back and hope it passed inspection. Any new-looking scratch or ding would be charged to Donovan. Then Donovan would catch a bus and come back to join Jack.

Lovell, Maris, and Emlyn climbed out of the van. Maris wore a corduroy jumper and looked thin and romantic, the high, squishy collar of her shirt showing off her slender throat. Lovell wore bright pink tights and a very pink, very large, very long sweater. Nobody could miss Lovell.

The three girls walked toward the impressive front entrance. A guard stood on the top of a retaining wall, his boots touching the flowers in their last bloom. He watched traffic, the two museum parking lots, and every person who came and went. There was no expression on his face. He paid no more attention to the girls than he did to the pigeons.

Emlyn used her Friends' card while Lovell and Maris paid to get in.

"We're here to see the film," said Lovell to the woman at the desk. Sunday afternoons the museum showed foreign films.

"That won't start for half an hour," the woman

said pleasantly. "You've time for a quick browse in the museum. Have you seen the current exhibit? On loan from Chicago? Early American oil portraits! It's quite wonderful. Here's a brochure."

"Oh, thank you!" said Lovell. "Early American oils! Wow."

The girls laughed and fell against each other and went on into Dinosaurs.

"They still don't have a tyrannosaurus rex," said Maris sadly. "There's only so much joy you can get out of a brontosaurus."

The guard had been leaning against the wall, but now he stood tall and walked toward them. "Hi," said Lovell, looking very pink. "We're here for the film. Are we headed the right way?"

He nodded and pointed.

He didn't look familiar to Emlyn, but it wouldn't have mattered much; he didn't really see her. Lovell and Maris were taking up all the space and interest. The guard had not come over because they looked suspicious. He came because they looked adorable.

Emlyn felt safe in her dull, middle-aged gray. And then, unexpectedly, a tremor shot from ankle to jaw, and her body quivered and ached. A little cry came out of her, and Lovell turned to look, while Maris talked more loudly to the guard.

Emlyn imagined him holding her against the wall, calling real police officers, being searched, handcuffed, placed in the backseat of a squad car, the way they showed on television, the officer's palm pushing her head down and in. She imagined the police showing up at the restaurant where her parents and their friends were lingering over coffee.

A twitch took over her kneecap, as if parts of her body wanted out. My bones are panicking, she thought. I have to stop considering right thing, wrong thing, and think *meaningless*. Just bones. I'm here for a bag of bones.

They finished Impressionist Paintings as quickly as any four-year-old. In the middle of the Sculpture Hall was a small silvery stand with a delicate arrow and a curly script sign that said FILMS.

Two heavyset women were standing by the arrow, discussing last Sunday's film and whether tonight's program was really worth waiting for.

Lovell checked her watch. "We have twenty-six minutes," she said clearly. "Let us broaden our minds. I suggest that we gaze upon Early American oil portraits."

"No," said Maris. "I want to see the mummy."

The middle-aged women smiled, and the girls left giggling, like junior high idiots whose slumber party lasted too long, and bobbled toward the Egyptian Room. Except that by the time Maris and Lovell reached the Egyptian Room, Emlyn would no longer be with them.

In the Great Hall, while Maris and Lovell kept their eyes open, Emlyn took out her key and approached the door marked MUSEUM OFFICIALS ONLY.

Lovell gasped when she saw the door marked SECURITY and yanked on Emlyn's sleeve to point it out to her.

"I saw," said Emlyn. This was the moment. Either she had a master key or she didn't. Her hair was prickling. The shudder of her scalp slithered down her arms, lifting her skin, peeling it away from her.

"It isn't too late," whispered Lovell, her eyes wide-open and scared. "We can still just forget it."

The thirst of fear had dried out Emlyn's mouth and throat. Even her thinking was dried out, as if she were in a sandstorm in the desert.

"My dad's a lawyer," breathed Maris, "if you need one."

"What do you mean, if *I* need one?" whispered Emlyn. "If *I* need a lawyer, we *all* need a lawyer."

"Right. I just meant — well — you have the phone number, right?"

Emlyn could not respond. They had been over this ten times. Anyway, she did not trust her voice. What if she agreed? What if she said, Yes, let's run, let's bag it, we're out of here?

Then her chance, her great and wonderful chance, would be over, and she would despise herself forever.

"Emlyn, what if somebody has gone into the office since you phoned?" whispered Lovell. "I mean, you phoned ten minutes ago, and just because nobody answered the secretary's line, and nobody answered the director's line, doesn't mean there isn't somebody in there now!"

Emlyn could not stand having to worry about Maris and Lovell and whether they followed through.

"Let's not," said Lovell in a regular voice. "I mean it. Come on, let's leave. This is too risky. This is downright stupid. We are all total jerks. We could — "

Emlyn pulled her sweater sleeves down to cover her hands. She slid the key into the lock. It fit. She pressed it to the right. It turned. The deadbolt snicked clear.

Lovell made a tiny moan.

"Go watch the doors!" Emlyn hissed. But they stood next to her, waiting. With her other sleeve-covered hand, Emlyn turned the knob and opened the door marked MUSEUM OFFICIALS ONLY.

She withdrew the key, slid into the darkness of the old mansion, and shut the door behind her.

It was as dark as a tomb.

It had a silent, dusty, half-occupied feeling.

But it was not a frightening dark. It was soft dark, like her own bedroom in the middle of the night. Emlyn leaned against the door, listening through the crack.

Lovell and Maris were supposed to move on, see the mummy, be regular people, and then go to the film and go home.

Lovell had done some cleaning crew investigation.

The museum was open Sunday from two to five and not open at all on Monday. There was no cleaning Sunday night. Weekend cleaning occurred Monday night. Sunday was the only night of the week when the lights would actually be off and the museum silent.

Presumably, since guards existed to keep the people from hurting or taking anything, there wouldn't be many on a Sunday after the museum closed. Lovell guessed that after the doors were shut at five, there would be sweeping and picking up of brochures and so forth left on benches, but the staff would be exhausted and looking forward to time off. Surely by six P.M. there would be nobody around.

Any remaining guard would have little to do. Surely he would wander only occasionally and without paying much attention. He would not tiptoe or creep. He'd just walk. The floors were stone. Emlyn would hear a guard coming.

Emlyn felt her way down the hall to the third door on the right, the room with desks and computers and stacked boxes of things. Its door, when she reached it, was neither closed nor locked. From a street lamp outside came a little light through a single window. The mansion sat very high on its foundation. Nobody could look in that window without a ladder. Emlyn sat at the rear desk, facing the door. Even if a guard brought a ladder and put his face up against the window, he would not see her. She was too far back and to the side.

If anybody came into the offices, she would hear the heavy metallic snick of the deadbolt. She would have time to slide to the floor and hide in the kneehole of the desk. It was inconceivable that the clerk who used this desk for storage would show up Sunday after closing.

She thought of Amaral-Re, quiet in her own dark. For Amaral-Re, it was always dark, for she had only painted eyes, and whatever was left of the girl herself was varnished solid.

I will touch her, thought Emlyn, and hold her and know her weight. She will be mine. And I, in some way, forevermore, will be hers.

She took her watch off, the better to stare at its fluorescent numbers, and sat silent and motionless while the minutes ticked.

She had hours to wait. Two hours of foreign film, one hour of letting staff filter away.

Three hours before her next move.

Nine

Six P.M.

The museum should be empty. Maris and
Lovell would have left by a theater exit, one of
the flat-to-the-wall doors with no handle on the
exterior. At this moment, not only should every
visitor be gone, so should every staff member.
Emlyn should be alone in this building except for
a guard or two.

Even so, she waited another forty-five minutes.

Her legs cramped. She felt as if she were on a
flight to nowhere, strapped to a hard, unfriendly
seat.

She put on her disposable gloves. They stuck to
her fingers. When she had practiced at home, in
the dark of her walk-in closet, she had found that
the gloves glowed a tiny bit in the dark, and so
she had decided on a second glove layer. Flexing

her fingers to make the plastic fit, she pulled her thin, supple knit gloves over them. She would leave no prints. She would not transfer her skin oils or bacteria to the mummy.

Slowly, she moved toward the door that opened into the Great Hall. She would stand with her ear pressed against the crack, waiting to hear a guard make his rounds. That was what guards did, wasn't it? Once he passed by, she would simply follow him, because he would not come back into the same room but make a circuit, the way museumgoers did. She ought to have plenty of time before he entered Egypt again. But once she began, Emlyn had to be quick, because the pedestal on which the mummy lay would be so very visibly empty on the guard's next tour.

Still, it did not seem to Emlyn that she could have less than an hour in which to work. She had pretended every bit of this at home in her bedroom, going nowhere, not even lifting her feet, but counting steps and seconds and writing them down. But no matter how carefully she timed everything, she really didn't know anything. She was only guessing that she could even get the Plexiglas cover off to start with.

She was desperate to get going. But she had to know that the guard was ahead of her and not behind her, and she could not leave the office until that had happened.

Seven ten. Seven thirty. Seven forty-five.

What if the guard watched TV someplace until midnight?

What if he didn't bother with rounds at all,

79

and she just stood here, hour after hour, her ear turning into the shape of a crack?

What if the guard sat next door, in the room marked SECURITY, his door open so he could watch the Great Hall while he sipped coffee and worked on a bag of jelly doughnuts?

She did silent exercises to keep from getting stiff.

They had decided that Lovell and Maris must go on home. Lovell must be at her house to talk to Emlyn's parents, should they call, which was impossible, they never had, but suppose they did.

Maris really did have to go home; they were having cousins over for dinner. She had to keep the baby happy while her aunt and uncle relaxed. "Though how I'm going to relax, I don't know," Maris had said.

Donovan and Jack would be in the van.

She wondered what they were talking about, or thinking. They had all realized that they would not know when she was going to burst out of the museum. They just had to be ready. It could be seven P.M. or ten P.M. Midnight or two in the morning.

The silence of the museum was broken by a horrific crash, metal against metal, like a car driving through the wall, like a sculpture falling from its niche. Emlyn almost cried out.

What could be wrong?

Should she go help? What on earth could have happened? She had absolutely no idea what that sound might have been.

It happened again.

The third time, she realized it must be the

clanging of the heavy iron grilles as the guard slammed them shut after himself. He didn't care how much noise he made. There was nobody here to hear it.

Now she could hear his steps.

The sound was so regular and so loud that each smack of his heels could have been a bullet. She had never dreamed how noisy it would be here. Was it the marble floors? The lack of carpet and drapes? Or did this man weigh two hundred fifty pounds, and was wearing boots with steel toes, hoping to crack a few tiles? Or a few heads?

Did he carry a club and a revolver along with his boredom? If he caught her, would he slam her against the wall just for something to do? Or was the guard a pleasant, tired, overweight woman with a particularly heavy gait?

I'll never know, she told herself. I'm not planning to let the guard see me, and he won't check in here because it's locked and

She had not locked the door after herself.

She had been so relieved that her key worked. So glad to get away from Lovell and Maris. So proud of herself for not giving in to her fears and running away from this adventure. So glad that it was dark and empty in the offices the way she had insisted to the other four that it would be. So relieved that the game had finally started and she was in.

I left it unlocked, she thought. I can't believe it. What a classic error. From Watergate to me.

She blushed in the dark.

The guard's eyes would be flitting from corner

to corner, shadow to shadow, door to door. Of course he would try this door. That was his job — to see that everything was locked!

She could turn the lock from the inside, but it would make that great, loud snick.

Should she hide? Should she scurry like a rat back to the desk's kneehole and hunch down? What if she banged into something in the hall? What if she couldn't find the right door in the dark? What if —

He was in the Great Hall. He could probably hear the creaking rasp of her desperate breathing.

But the footsteps came no closer. They faded without a break in rhythm. Just the pacing of somebody slow and dull. Somebody who had walked this a thousand times and would walk it a thousand more and no longer even saw what he was looking at, because an empty museum was always the same as it had been a minute ago.

The steps changed sound, adding a slight shuffle. A minor scrape.

He was going up the stairs.

After ten minutes, she opened the door a crack and nearly cried out.

The Great Hall was not dark.

She almost slammed the door shut again but caught it with an inch to go. It had never occurred to her that there might be lights on. The inchwide opening revealed very little. She had to step out, still half in the safety of the door, and look at this lighting.

The museum had night-lights. Close to the

82

floor were low-wattage bulbs that cast a friendly yellow light.

She had pictured herself sliding through darkness like a cat through an alley. But no. The pale walls took on the shadows of every object, because the light came from the bottom and nothing could escape. Her dark clothes would make her stand out.

There was nothing she could do now unless she took Lovell's advice and quit. She could slide back into the office, go to the exit door she had chosen, and fly across the street to the safety of the van. They would accept whatever she said. "There are guards everywhere — it won't work — we were wrong. Drive away fast!" she could cry to Jack and Donovan.

But there were not guards everywhere. She could no longer hear the feet of the one guard. Do it! she said to herself. You weren't afraid of the dark. Do not be afraid of the light.

Very slowly, she shut the door marked MUSEUM OFFICIALS ONLY behind her and carefully turned the key. This time the lock did not snick quite so loud. Perhaps her double gloves had muffled it. She put the key safely in her pocket and patted it for comfort.

The stairs were so wide. So exposed. You could walk four abreast up these stairs. But you could not see what was at the top; the high banisters hid your view. Emlyn just had to walk up, trusting that no guard was waiting for her.

She took each step as softly and quickly as she could.

When she got toward the top she crouched a little, trying to see but not be seen.

How open it was! By day, she had been sure there were hiding places. By night, she saw that there were none. The dark corners were lit, the floor gleamed like mirrors, and the circulating confusion of children and the press of visitors did not exist.

If the guard returned, her only choice would be to stand still and hope.

She crept between huge glass walls of stuffed bison, forever grazing on painted prairie. Then, changing continents in a single step, she entered Egypt.

The mummy lay in the center of the room, staring at the ceiling. She looked frail and breakable in the half-light.

Emlyn could imagine her alive; trying to stay alive; trying to catch one last breath; trying to say one last word. And then, the embalmers. Turning an innocent girl as flat and thin and dry as old paper. The eternal tightness of bandages, the eternal emptiness where they cut out her lifelines and poured them into jars.

Amaral. Such a beautiful name.

Emlyn worked her fingernails under the Plexiglas. The slippery rubber against her skin felt funny, especially because it was invisible under the knit gloves. Her nails were strong and thick, and she easily worked the big rectangular aquarium-like case off its wooden pier. Bracing herself, she inched around the four sides, walking it upward.

Without sound and without slippage, she got one narrow end all the way up. She edged around, got a good grip, and picked up the whole thing. It was good that she was accustomed to lifting boats.

She raised it in the air and then over her head, as if she and it were going out on the river together. She was panting from the weight and the angle. She carried it a few steps, slid it down, and rested it on her toes to keep it from slamming on the floor. Carefully, she tilted it back and forth and into a safe place against the wall. She did not think she had made a single sound.

Amaral continued to lie motionless. Her painted eyes did not blink, and her hidden arms did not wave.

Emlyn stared down into her face, fighting the urge to rip off her gloves and feel Amaral, feel that linen, its threads, and its woven corners. Run her own bare skin over the gold paint that had encircled Amaral's head before there was a city of Rome, before there was an English language, before ships had crossed the sea to the New World.

Propped in tiny wooden slots on the mummy's slab were the cards that told her history. Emlyn brushed accidently against them, and when they fluttered to the floor she saw that one card had been hidden behind another.

She could not resist picking it up, but it resisted capture, because her gloves were not able to get under it. Finally she had it in her hands.

In the same brown ink, the same spidery,

square handwriting, was a quote from an ancient Egyptian letter. A personal letter, although not one Amaral-Re had sent.

My heart has stolen forth and goes quietly to a place it knows well.

Had Amaral had time in her life to fall in love and lose her love? To steal forth and seek the company of a place she knew well?

Amaral's real heart, the organ that had pumped blood through her, would still be within her bones. For Amaral's heart would be judged when she tried to reach eternity: The gods would stand beside her and weigh her heart against a feather, and if her sins and acts of cruelty and wrong were great, the feather would know, and Amaral would not find eternal life.

Emlyn considered her readings. Philosophy and religion discussed death at length. But Emlyn was not concerned with death. She was concerned with a body. How sacred was a body? Was it sacred for just a few years?

Would Amaral-Re have been sacred for, say, a decade? Or a century? But now was not? Was the body just something to shove under glass? After thirty centuries, had the body ceased to be sacred? Not to an ancient Egyptian.

Amaral's family laid her to rest with the hope of eternal life. That life required her body and her bones. Inside her wrappings would be amulets designed to protect her from evil.

Evil, thought Emlyn. Will I be the one who is evil, taking her into danger?

Ancient Egyptians were a people who were sure. They knew exactly what death was: It was life all over again, along the Nile, complete with servants. Amaral-Re's mummy here in a dull little city in the United States seemed proof that the ancients were wrong.

But maybe not. Maybe they just had the wrong time frame. In which case, Asmaral-Re would still require her body.

Emlyn read the card again and then tucked it into the upper, inside pocket of the blazer. Stop it, she told herself. You don't need a souvenir.

But she did.

She wanted something to keep, and they were not keeping the mummy.

Don't take it, she said to herself. That's how people get caught, they keep things from the scene.

But no. Only Emlyn knew this card existed. It had been caught behind another card for decades. It was her secret now and Amaral's. *My heart has stolen forth and goes quietly to a place it knows well.* The place Emlyn would know well was the memory of possessing Amaral-Re for a night.

Emlyn slid her hands under Amaral's shoulders. Emlyn had had a nightmare in which Amaral's bones fell free, and Emlyn had to scoop them back up and stuff them back in. But the mummy felt solid.

She pulled her fingers back, took off her blazer, and rolled up her left sleeve. The two black bags peeled away in a moment. She edged one bag around the mummy's lower extremity, the way you would slide a pillow into its case. Properly, Emlyn could call this the mummy's feet, but you could not tell there were two of anything

87

inside all that wrapping: It was more of a rising right triangle at the bottom of the body.

The mummy did not feel like dried bones in a sheet, and she did not feel like papier-mâché, which crumbled and broke at a touch. She felt like plaster. Emlyn did not have to worry that Amaral would bend in the middle and ask for a wheelchair.

The first bag went up to the mummy's shoulders. Ripping tape off her right sleeve, Emlyn secured the bag as if with suspenders, up and over the shoulders and head of the mummy. Then she slid the second bag over the head and taped that closed at the knees.

Gauging the best place to distribute the weight, she lifted Amaral a little above the middle, and concentrating, taking a solid stance, found her own center of gravity. Then she raised her arms until Amaral was over her head like a canoe. We're good to go, Amaral, she said silently to her silent captive.

If the guard came now, she would have no explanation except the real one. Yes. I'm stealing your mummy.

Emlyn was grateful this time for the night-lights. Her load was not awkward because she was used to that sort of shape and weight, although definitely Amaral weighed more than the thirty-pound scull.

The stairs were difficult.

To balance a mummy on the head while moving blindly down steps wasn't easy. Emlyn had not stopped to think that the plastic bags would slide around. She was not holding rough linen that would have given traction. She was holding thin, slippery plastic that she had not fastened tightly. If she took the tiniest misstep she was going to lose her grip, and the mummy would shoot out of her hands and down these huge stairs.

Emlyn kept her thigh against the inside wall of the stair in order to keep herself upright.

When she reached the glittering marble floor of the Great Hall she saw the door marked SECURITY and her heart clenched. She had meant to take the freight elevator down. What was she doing on the stairs? The guard could be in that very room, coming or going this very moment, and she was sauntering in front of him with the mummy?

I can't even remember the strategies I've planned for days, she thought, the strategy I went over a hundred times sitting at that desk in the office.

So now she knew that tension erased thought. It was fine to have plans. But if you forgot them, they did you little good.

Shaking, exhausted, she transferred Amaral's weight to her shoulder. The tape ripped free of the bags, and for a horrible second Emlyn was holding nothing but bag: The mummy was sliding out.

Desperately, Emlyn caught, and scrabbled, and made a save.

She thought she could fish the key out of her pocket with one hand while balancing the mummy with the other, but it was impossible. Amaral was much heavier than Emlyn had expected and growing heavier by the moment.

She braced herself, and leaning to the side, got Amaral's feet on the floor. It would have been easier to stand her on her head, but Emlyn couldn't do that. Forget Amaral's dignity, Emlyn told herself. She has no dignity, she's a mummy. You can stand her any old way. She won't know.

Emlyn straightened, straightening Amaral, too, and the vertical mummy gave a small, short clatter.

Up inside her, something had fallen loose.

Oh, no, thought Emlyn. Her bones? Did a vertebra or a rib just land at her ankles?

It was funny, in a sick sort of way, but Emlyn did not have time to think about falling bones. She crossed the room, unlocked the door, carried the slippery Amaral in just as the bottom bag tore free, leaned the mummy against the wall, scooped up the puddle of black plastic, closed the door, and locked it.

Then she leaned against the door and swallowed several times. She was dangerously close to throwing up. So many errors. Major acts of stupidity. She imagined the terrible, destructive crash of the mummy smashing into the marble.

For some time, there was only the sound of her own breathing.

No footsteps, no doors opening, no grilles slamming, no distant radio, no nothing.

Emlyn looked at her watch. It had taken eleven minutes.

It was probably some kind of record for stealing a mummy.

She had lots more tape. This time when she

put Amaral into her bag, she taped it around the waist and knees as well, so it could not slip as much. It was surprisingly easy to do in the dark. Tightness was something your fingers knew, not your eyes.

At the planning sessions, Donovan and Jack had thought she was being sentimental and emotional to waste time worrying about bags. "It's just a thing," Jack had said. "So what if somebody spills Coke on it? Skip the garbage bags."

"She wants the dark of it," Lovell had said.

"It won't be dark, because it's plastic, and plastic shines," Donovan had argued.

Emlyn and the mummy made their way down the hall and once more into the office under whose desk she had sat those three hours. There was the door that faced the street where the van was parked.

She rested Amaral-Re against the wall. She had been scrupulous about not using her flashlight, but when she felt her way to the door she couldn't find it. There was streetlight coming through the window, but somehow it didn't illuminate the door. She knelt on the floor, keeping the bulky desk between herself and the window, and turned her light on. When she felt in control of the slender beam, she crept over to the door, as beautifully carved as she remembered, and led the beam along the door to the handle.

There wasn't one.

Emlyn blinked. Her heart went cold. Inside her double gloves her joints hurt.

She looked around her. She was exactly where she had planned to be. This was the door she had picked out. She had checked inside and out-side.

She ran her hands around the door.

It had been stripped of its hardware and sealed.

It was only a door on the outside, keeping the integrity of the mansion. On the inside, it was just a pretty wall.

This was not a door.

She couldn't get out.

Ten

Calm down, she said to herself. Calm down. There are other doors, I counted them on the outside of the mansion. I chose this door because I was sure it wouldn't be connected to an alarm, and at least I'm right about that. I'm locked in. I'm stupid, but I'm right.

At the end of the hall was the door the secretary used when she had her cigarette. Emlyn did not walk toward it. It opened onto a different block than the one where the van was parked. Whereas the van was on a true side street, without traffic, that other door opened onto a major intersection. Maybe at three in the morning she could go out that way, but it was barely eight thirty. There would be cars and witnesses everywhere. She couldn't bump out that door with a mummy on her shoulder.

And that door was certain to be wired to the alarms, and there she'd be, not with a single two-lane street to cross but with a block and a half to walk and a much-heavier-than-expected mummy on her shoulder.

Okay.

Check the other doors.

There were two more, each inside a separate office. She would have to unlock those offices, check to see if those outside doors worked, bring the mummy —

You can do it, she said to herself. This is a minor little fluff of a problem. Okay. Don't drag the mummy around. Put her in the hall, find a door, come back for her.

She felt like two people: the terrified loser who didn't know what to do, and the coach giving instructions and pep talks.

She lifted Amaral straight up, like a department store mannequin she planned to set in the window, and bizarrely, she could feel Amaral-Re's elbow in her side, as if they were girlfriends poking each other. How strange. Shouldn't there be enough padding so you couldn't feel separate bones? Amaral's arms must not be straight down at her sides but folded on her chest. Somehow it seemed a more comfortable eternity to have your arms folded than to have them straight and bound by your sides. You were less of a prisoner all those centuries.

From inside Amaral-Re's shroud came a little metallic scrape. It was not the same as the previous little clunk.

Emlyn felt her eyes glaze.

What had moved?

Bones shifting?

Some dreadful insect chewing?

Emlyn steadied herself, gripping the heavy doorjamb of the Trustees' Room. It was the kind of molding that craftsmen had worked on for months, when the mansion was being built. It felt solid and sure under her fingers.

The floor in the hallway was dark wood, polished to a rich and beautiful gleam.

It was also slippery. The combination of slick plastic bag against glossy wood was too much. The mummy would not stand upright. The moment Emlyn let go, Amaral slid out from under herself. Emlyn did not want to jostle the mummy anymore. She could not be slinging her around like some bag of groceries.

Emlyn put the mummy against the wall, supporting her on one side with a chair that must be for people who didn't deserve to sit in the Trustees' Room. On the other side, she dragged over an immense potted plant. She patted her pocket for the key in case she had to unlock the exit door, in case it was not a push-bar safety exit. The sharp, used-only-once jags in the key's edge felt strong and sure, even through her double gloves.

Halfway down the office hall she stumbled and dropped the key. She knelt, trying to find it, swiping the tiny ray of the flashlight back and forth. The key was not visible.

"Oh, I think so, I completely agree," said

the strong, intense voice of Harris Brisband.

From the Great Hall came the smack of heavy feet on marble floors.

Emlyn scrambled up without finding her key and put out her flashlight.

There was the distinct slotting sound of a key going into its hole.

Dr. Brisband was about to unlock MUSEUM OFFICIALS ONLY, and she was standing in his hall with a stolen mummy.

She had one second in which to vanish. One second in which he would seize the knob, turn it, open the door, and see a huge black plastic bag containing his mummy.

Almost dead herself, Emlyn yanked open the bathroom door and slid in, but she ran out of time before she could close it all the way. She stood in the dark next to the sink, fingers gripping the inside knob, pressing the door up to the lock but not into it.

The hall lights came on.

Male voices continued.

The men were speaking English, but she was so horrified she had to reinterpret it. She shivered and again almost threw up.

"Look at this," said Dr. Brisband irritably. "They can't even take the trash out to the Dumpster. It's impossible to get good cleaning help. We had our own staff; it was a miserable failure. We tried private contracting; that was worse. We've gone back to our own cleaning crew, and I was beginning to feel hopeful — and look at this. Garbage stuffed behind a plant next to the Trustees' Room. After you, Bob."

She could see the shadow of Dr. Brisband ushering Bob forward. She heard another lock click and another door open. They were going inside Dr. Brisband's office.

Shut the door after you, prayed Emlyn.

They went inside. They did not shut the door after themselves.

This was when Emlyn knew that if anything goes wrong, a thousand things go wrong. Huge blocks of wrong, tumbling down on you like a collapsing pyramid.

She had to get out of here while he still thought that was trash. There was no question of hiding in the kneehole of a desk now. When the guard came around again and found the mummy missing, he would shoot down here to tell Dr. Brisband, and they would figure out what the trash was. They would certainly figure out that the person who had taken the mummy was right there next to it.

She would go down the freight elevator, out into the service courtyard, and through its exit into the street. Of course then she'd have to walk around the entire museum block with the mummy in her arms in order to reach the van.

The van. It felt as if she had been here for years. It felt as if Jack and Donovan might have finished high school and gone on to college by now. She prayed that they were still waiting for her.

Forget the mummy, she said to herself. Just get your own body out of here.

She eased the bathroom door open another few inches. Dr. Brisband's office door was wide open. Its slant prevented her from seeing inside and presumably prevented them from seeing out, as well.

How long would they be in there?

She heard the sound of a computer booting up and the singing cues of a program coming on. A few clicks. A pause. Another click, a whirr, and the distinct sound of pages. He was printing something out.

"There you go, Bob," said Dr. Brisband.

"Glad I could help," said Bob, which sounded incorrect to Emlyn. If Dr. Brisband was printing out the information, he was the one helping.

The two men came out of Dr. Brisband's office without having turned off the computer or the printer. "This is just right," said Bob.

They began a long, detailed good-bye, standing in the door to the Great Hall. Bob would see Dr. Brisband at the board meeting next week. Bob fully supported Dr. Brisband's position. But the votes did not look good.

Emlyn was close enough that she could have joined the conversation. She pressed her eyes closed and her lips together to keep from repeating that awful little whimper she had made hours ago in front of Lovell.

Bob departed. Dr. Brisband returned to his office. Again he failed to close his door. The light from his room spilled into the hall.

There lay her key.

Far from being swallowed up into the brown floor, it seemed to glow and pulse with a brassy stare. How could Dr. Brisband have missed it?

Emlyn stood motionless, except for her panting. The key seemed a football field away. She knew it was only six or eight steps.

Dr. Brisband began muttering to himself. He was sending e-mails. "And Susan," he mumbled. "She'll help. And Aaron. Definitely Richard."

Go, Emlyn coached herself. Go now.

She slipped into the hall. She knelt, so rattled that she didn't stoop in the right place and had to crawl to reach the key. She tucked it back into her pants pocket.

" San Francisco," mumbled Dr. Brisband. "Boston. London."

Keep sending, thought Emlyn. Think donor, think board meeting. Just don't turn around and think about me.

She inched the potted plant away from the mummy. There was nothing between her and Dr. Brisband except a shadow. She picked the mummy up. It did not resemble trash waiting to be tossed, it was far too solid and vertical. On the other hand, she knew what was in it, and Dr. Brisband did not.

So far.

Her sneakers made a tiny squeak on the wooden floor, and she imagined herself sounding like a whole basketball team racing out, sneakers shrieking.

She held Amaral in her arms, only a few inches into the air, took ten steps down the hall, turned, opened the door that took her into the hallway with the freight elevator. Closing that door behind her required holding the mummy, maneuvering in total dark, praying that the lock would not make a racket, and apologizing to God for praying about a criminal act.

In the dark, she felt around the wall until she found the light switch and clicked it. There were no windows for anybody to watch her through. She was almost crippled by the size and weight of Amaral in her arms. She pushed the elevator button.

The elevator was old and noisy. It creaked and rasped and clattered. It was not going to be a secret when Emlyn chose a floor. Would Dr. Brisband come running? Would he know that absolutely nobody should be using that elevator right now? Or would he think, Oh, good, it's our Sunday night delivery.

Did the guard use this elevator? Would the door open and the guard step forward?

Hi, Emlyn would say. Just taking the trash out.

So once inside this elevator, assuming it was empty, did she go up to the second floor, unbag Amaral, put her back, and hide out in the bathrooms until the public was allowed back in?

The cleaning crew would be back in first: Monday night.

And long before them, Maris or Lovell or Jack or Donovan would have panicked and told somebody or done something.

Not to mention her parents. They never checked on her because she always got home. But if she *didn't* get home, they would check. Her parents were relentless once they put their minds to something. Five minutes of interrogation, and Lovell and Maris would spill everything.

Not my daughter, her father would say.

Yes, your daughter.

Her father had almost collapsed this summer when Emlyn's younger brother was caught in the liquor cabinet and had to admit he'd been taking quite a few sips in the last few months. And Emlyn's mother had wept for weeks last year when the same brother shoplifted a video-tape.

She thought of the desperate love of parents, trying to surround you and wrap you and teach you, but not really knowing you. Just blundering along, trying. Counting on you.

She thought of being caught and facing them, two people she loved who counted on her.

Or . . . Emlyn could take the elevator to the basement and keep going, blindly and stupidly hoping to rescue herself. If she gave up now, she would definitely be caught and her parents would definitely know. If she kept going, she had a chance.

The big shiny brown elevator doors slid into the wall, and from inside the elevator, dark, curly fingers reached for Emlyn. She managed to stop herself before a scream came out of her. It was a plastic tree sitting in the corner, a touch of fake nature.

She got in with the tree and her mummy and pressed B, which she hoped stood for basement.

The elevator sounded like her future: falling and groaning and splitting apart. It stopped with a thud, and the doors opened slowly and remorselessly. She had no idea what would be down here.

Darkness. That was what was down here. Complete, total, solid dark.

She got out of the elevator, so tired from fright she could hardly bump Amaral out of the elevator.

The doors slid closed, and she was alone in a basement in the dark with a mummy.

Eleven

Emlyn turned on her flashlight.

A huge scarlet mouth and a face dripping with greasy gray hair lunged at her.

She whimpered and tried to scrabble back into the elevator, but she could not find the buttons. She clung to the mummy as if Amaral-Re could protect her, as if those hieroglyphs painted on her linens were magic spells. Emlyn's tears spattered on the black plastic that held Amaral.

It was a mask.

A huge, hanging mask, three or four feet tall. She recognized it, actually. There was such a mask in the Polynesian Room, so the museum must have an extra or a double and didn't display it, but just hung it down here.

The thin, hard beam of her flashlight showed statues, crates, racks of costumes; old textiles and paintings and pieces off things; rugs rolled up and empty picture frames leaning against one another. There was a row of ancient bicycles, the kind where the front wheel was taller than the rider and the back wheel just a toy. An old-fashioned square piano with the ivory peeling off the keys even had a piece of sheet music waiting to be played.

Just storage, she said to herself. Whatever they're not exhibiting this week. Or not exhibiting ever. None of it matters. Don't even look. Find the way out.

On the wall about two feet from the elevator buttons, her flashlight revealed switches. A whole row. Unlabeled. Did she dare turn those on? Upstairs in SECURITY, would a signal register that somebody was in the basement?

A museum that failed to fasten its mummy down didn't seem likely to have such technology, but who knew?

In spite of the careful taping, Amaral-Re slid inside her bags. She was rattling with every step Emlyn took. What if the mummy had to lie flat or disintegrate? This mummy had been lying flat for three thousand years. What if Emlyn was killing her right now? And by the time she got to the van, Amaral-Re, princess, would be nothing but a bolt of stained cloth and a pile of bones?

She could leave the mummy here in the basement. They would find Amaral tomorrow, or at least eventually, and put her back, and the damage would be minimal.

But it was one thing to be slid down a gleaming limestone tunnel for eternal rest in your own pyramid as your servants wailed and your family wept and your priesthood sang. It was quite another to be tossed into a cellar in trash bags.

Emlyn took a deep breath.

This wasn't field hockey, but it had a certain resemblance. She was halfway into the game and hadn't scored. Both her offense and her defense had been pretty slack. But the game wasn't over. She still wanted to win.

She did not turn on the lights.

Her flash had been strong enough for a small office. It was no more than the light of a struck match in this enormous cellar.

She was sure of only one thing. Any door would be on a wall. She had to follow the walls to find a way out. But that was easy to deduce and hard to accomplish.

Things had been jumbled and pushed and stacked and added. Little room had been left for moving around, and in some cases no room. Emlyn couldn't pass through. And if she could squeeze her own slim body between artifacts, she couldn't bring Amaral.

She had to carry Amaral on her shoulder, which meant that each end of the mummy risked hitting some crate or hanging object.

Portraits, boxes, shelving stuck in the middle and filled with vases or dishes. Furniture, hats, glass trays of pinned butterflies.

This was where they stuck what they were never going to want. People thinking how generous they were to give their grandmother's wedding gown to the museum, but to the museum it was just one more fragile thing to hang up and worry about. And forget about.

The flashlight's path was so narrow that she had to point around the edges of things to figure out what they were. She could balance Amaral for only a moment with one hand, catching brief, slanted glimpses of things and hoping to find a path through the chaos, and then she had to put her flashlight hand back up to support the mummy. In the end, she had to carry Amaral vertically and hope Amaral's bones would hold.

Leaning against an old heart-painted blanket chest was an immense, antique black-and-white photograph. It was an excellent shot. Scrambling up huge blocks — a giant's blocks — a great, impossible tower of pale, shining children's blocks — was a man in dated safari clothing. She stared for several moments before she realized it was a pyramid he was climbing. He might even be the very tourist, and future museum founder, who had acquired Amaral-Re.

She had not known how huge blocks in pyramids were.

She had not known you could climb them like that, scrambling, reaching, stretching, risking a terrible fall.

She closed her eyes against the deep, heavy dark of the basement, and something else deep and heavy took hold and Emlyn fell into a hot blast of sun off those blocks. The blinding reflection and the blistering heat charred her thoughts. How dry the wind. She, too, would be a husk, left out in this sand to dry.

Gripping the elbows of Amaral-Re, Emlyn felt herself hung with gold: gold bands on her wrist, gold belt around her waist, gold amulet at her throat, gold rings on her toes. The gold weighted her down, pulling her under. She could not get out of the sun.

"No," Emlyn mumbled, "I'm here, not there." She pulled herself up into the dark and the dust.

If I spend any longer in this place, dreaming of papyrus and pyramids, I will go a little bit insane, and they will find me someday, mummified in a corner, under a mask, thought Emlyn.

Where does this come from? I'm a sensible person. I have a sensible family. We read *Consumer Reports* before we purchase a car or microwave. Our meals are balanced and we exercise frequently. We are not reincarnated from Egyptian royalty. We do not time travel. We floss. We do not even mislay our remote controls.

Emlyn felt in need of a little remote control. If she could slow everything in the museum down, slow herself down, slow her heartbeat and her skipping brain, she could still make this work.

There, behind carpets hung like giant towels from giant dowels, was the soft pink of neon. EXIT. It was a regular door, not a bulkhead, and she was grateful. She had imagined opening two slanting metal doors of a bulkhead, and Dr. Brisband would be looking out his window and see her rising eerily in the moonlight with her mummy.

She worked her way toward the pink neon. The area in front of the door was entirely clear, and in fact a wide path extended from the EXIT door into the clutter of the basement. It led in a straight line to another door. Definitely not the way Emlyn had come in.

She flashed her light all around the windowless exit. There were no signs proclaiming that alarms would go off if the door opened. There was not a handle but a bar against which a person carrying something heavy, such as a mummy, could shove her hip and get out without needing to use hands.

Emlyn pressed the bar.

Please let it open.

Please let it open to some nice quiet dark place.

Please let it have a route to Jack and Donovan.

The door opened quietly and easily. No bells rang. No sirens squealed.

Emlyn peered out. Once again, there was a lot less dark than she had hoped for. The utility courtyard was lit by high, strong lights that sputtered to themselves, as if infested by bumblebees.

There were two parked cars alongside the museum van and a truck-sized trash container. Down the wall to her right was a lit window. As far as she could tell, its shade was pulled. She couldn't see into anything.

Two cars. One for Dr. Brisband? One for a guard? Was that the ratio of good guys to bad guys? Two against one? Emlyn ought to be able to outwit two people at a time.

She had not had a second in which to think about what she had accomplished so far, but now that she could breathe fresh air, and imagine escape from the museum, she thought, I did outwit the guard. I did outwit Dr. Brisband.

And then she thought, But I'm taking so long. Wasting time with dreams and silly pats on the back. It isn't my time that matters. It's the guard's time. Is he this very instant staring down in disbelief at the empty pedestal? Am I going to hear sirens the moment I step outside?

And just because there are only two cars doesn't mean there are only two people here. A hundred other guards could have parked on the street.

She and the mummy eased out, Emlyn keeping a toe in the door so it wouldn't close. There was the terrible possibility that she could not get out of the courtyard, either, and would have to go back into the basement and find another route. She could not let the basement door lock after her.

She had expected the basement to be below ground, but now that she thought about it, you had to go up a lot of steps to get into the building's main floor, steps on which she had sat and had ice cream and waited for people. But she'd been too dumb to analyze this. The first floor was high. So the basement was not a basement but a ground-level storage area. She emerged onto the truck-high cement walkway she'd seen from the road.

The garage door was marked by red reflectors.

She could not see any other door, although she knew there was one. She could not walk around the entire enclosure feeling for cracks. Especially not with a mummy in her arms. Especially with time running away from her.

She looked at the lit windows. Still blurry, definitely covered in some way.

There were no handy rocks or sticks with which to prop open the door. She took off one black glove and wedged it between the door and its lock.

She thought hard.

People got careless, and this was a careless museum to begin with. They did not have alarms, they did not have grilles at every opening, they did not frequently examine every room every night. They hired secretaries who talked too much and guards who just assumed that an office door that ought to be locked was locked.

And so it was just possible that the museum van had been left open.

Because it was quickest and because she could not use up more precious seconds, Emlyn lifted Amaral once more, carrying her horizontally on her shoulder, and walked straight across the parking area right under the blazing lights.

She had guessed right. They were counting on the courtyard for security. The driver's door of the van was not locked.

She opened the driver's door, leaned up, and tapped the automatic garage door opener with her finger. Then she shut the van door and ran across the entire, wide-open, well-lit asphalt to the garage door. It clattered and clanked — and opened, rising upward.

Emlyn ran as if she were carrying the scull to the river, as if there were a whole team with her, as if they were all yelling to raise her own excitement, as if there were no mummy and no museum and no danger and no drowning in gold.

She ducked out into the street. She was on the

far side of the museum and had to circle two long blocks to get back to the van. She ran.

I'm out, I'm out, I'm out! she screamed in her head. I have the mummy! I did it! I'm safe!

But she was not safe.

Emlyn ran the block, turned the corner, ran harder. She was now running past the windows of the mansion, and should Dr. Brisband look out, he would see — what?

Just a moving shape. Neither boy nor girl. As for the mummy, it would just be a thing.

She was falling apart.

Not the mummy. Emlyn. She was starting to sob, and she could not afford the breath or the breakdown. Her wrist felt rebroken and her shoulder dislocated. Her head ached and her fingers could hang on no longer.

She must get to the van.

The rows of parked cars seemed impenetrable. She had not looked at her watch in ages. Was it two in the morning? Or were people still having dinner and strolling around the block and getting in and out of their cars?

There was the van.

She darted between cars parked on her side, crossed the street, and got safely to the far sidewalk. Now there were two rows of parked cars between her and the museum. She did not see how she could support the weight of the mummy another step, but she had a half block to go. She was staggering, lurching, and the mummy was sliding inside its bag and blistering her shoulder, and then the side door of the van slid open and hands reached out to help.

Twelve

"Houston!" yelled Jack, à la space launches. "We have a mummy!"

They rested the mummy flat on the floor, her head behind the front passenger seat and her feet pressed up against the rear bench.

Jack threw his arms around Emlyn, no mean feat in the cramped van with the floor occupied. He hugged her exuberantly.

"Tell us everything!" demanded Donovan. He kissed her on the forehead and then on the cheek.

"Open the bag," said Jack.

"We thought you'd never get here!" said Donovan.

"We've been crazy with worry," said Jack. "We've been on the phone every ten minutes with Maris and Lovell for advice."

"Get going," said Emlyn. "Now. I had to open

the automatic garage door to get out. They know somebody was there who shouldn't have been there. They just don't know yet what I did. But they will. In one minute."

"Right," said Jack. "Right."

He was so excited he ground the gears and the car sounded like wounded lions.

The cars ahead and behind had parked so tightly that he had to maneuver back and forth and back and forth to get out, with Donovan yelling, "Don't hit them! We can't have an accident right now! Watch what you're doing! Can't you drive?"

"Shut up, Donovan! Whose van is this, anyway?"

Emlyn curled up on the floor next to Amaral. The van had thick carpeting, which on her orders Jack had vacuumed thoroughly. She hadn't wanted the mummy to pick up mud and grit from their shoes.

She peeled back some tape and gently folded up the black plastic.

A square of woven linen was exposed in the middle of black plastic, as if Amaral were a patient going in for surgery. The bandages had been woven log-cabin style, intricately, beautifully. Emlyn touched the linen. Then she took off her knit glove and her two disposable gloves and for the first time actually touched Amaral-Re. The cloth was harsher than she had expected, more like canvas than a handkerchief.

I stole a mummy, thought Emlyn.

A terrible, inexplicable horror seized her, and for a moment she was afraid she would begin sobbing and have to cling to the mummy for comfort.

She sat up quickly, got a Coke from the cooler, popped it open, and had a sip. Not letting herself look again, she tucked the plastic back. Then she checked her watch.

Eight fifty-one.

All that time. A lifetime, it had seemed, of fear and stupidity. And it was still early.

"Okay, here's the interstate, we're safe, we're out," Donovan told her.

Jack accelerated up the ramp. "We got so scared for you," he said. "There's been all this activity in the museum. There was some kind of event at the theater we didn't know about. It wasn't on the museum calendar, so it must have been private. Probably fifty people went into the theater long after Maris and Lovell were home from the film."

"*And*," said Donovan, "it turns out there's a guard who walks around the *outside* of the museum! We saw him *twice*."

Emlyn's heart shriveled. Pure luck he wasn't waiting for me on the other side of the garage door. Pure luck I didn't run smack into him while I was racing around the block.

"And then when we saw the director pull up!" said Donovan. "We had heart attacks. We thought of telephoning you on your cell phone, but we figured, it rings in there and she's dead."

Emlyn imagined her phone ringing while she was hiding in the bathroom and Dr. Brisband and his friend Bob were booting up the computer a few feet away. She couldn't laugh. "How did you know it was Dr. Brisband?"

"Just a guess. But a new four-door Mercedes? Vanity plates," said Jack, "that say MUSEUM? Sounds like a director to me."

The front had two bucket seats, Jack driving, Donovan the passenger. She knelt in the opening between the seats. "Where are we?"

"Going north on the interstate. We'll get off at exit 65, and then it's eight miles to my grandparents' cottage," said Donovan.

"You're sure they won't be there?"

"They're in Florida. They don't usually go down till after Thanksgiving — they're afraid of hurricanes this time of year — but friends of theirs are having a fiftieth anniversary celebration. The cottage is empty."

She was sweaty in a strange, cold way. What if she had left a trace in the office and they located her? What if a camera in some corner had photographed her? What if that outside guard had seen her get in this van and written down the plate number?

"I can't wait to see the mummy," said Jack. "There's a truck stop, I'm going to pull in there and open her up."

"No," said Emlyn. She put her hand on the part of the mummy that must be her head. Even though she wasn't going to let Jack see the mummy, she had to. She turned around and gently worked the plastic back up again, all the way to the top. Jack was too busy driving to see and Donovan too busy talking.

He was on the car phone with Maris and Lovell. "In the van!" he kept saying. "We've got the mummy *in the van!*" as if this were impossible to comprehend. "No, we don't have details yet. Emlyn has to catch her breath. Yes, I'll tell her. Em, Lovell says you're awesome. Maris says ten thousand congratulations."

In the soft, changing dark of the car, sudden quick light from the highway overheads darting in and darting out of the windows, the mummy was extraordinary.

Her face was larger than life. Her eyes, dark and sad, had far more makeup on them than Emlyn had seen through the old, discolored, scratched case. The gold leaf of her ornaments was so much more beautiful. Emlyn touched, and it was gold, even the tip of her finger knew it was gold. Nothing so rich and deep could be painted. The magnificence of Amaral-Re went through Emlyn's skin and into her soul.

What have I done? This girl, this work of art. This thing of beauty. I have thrown her into the back of a van with two punks who'd use her for a picnic bench. Who intend to string her up like a scarecrow so four hundred seniors can get ten minutes' kick out of her.

The realness of Amaral-Re was horrifying. Emlyn covered her again. She thought, What do I mean, *two* punks? I think *I'm* a good guy?

She had complete, sick knowledge of herself, the one to whom you were supposed to be true.

"Give me your seat, Donovan. I have to see where I'm going. I've spent a whole night with no idea where I'm going, and I want to read road signs. Be careful where you step. Amaral is very fragile."

"You make her sound like your girlfriend,"

Donovan teased. He climbed over into the middle swivel chair, and she took the front seat. The normalcy of turnpike signs and gas station signs and fast-food restaurant signs took away some of her anxiety. The city receded.

If they do have a photograph of me, it won't be long before they come for me. Dr. Brisband and his secretary will recognize me as the high school girl who made the appointment. They don't have my right name or my right school, but it's just a matter of showing the photograph to the principals. My principal sure knows me. His daughter lettered in crew last year when I did. "What if they catch me?" she said softly.

"How could they?"

"What if there was a hidden camera?"

The boys were silent for a while.

Then Jack said, "I don't think the museum would want the publicity. I think they'd just want their mummy back. They won't want people to know how easily a mere high school kid got in and out with a precious artifact. I bet they won't go to the police. If they do have a photograph, and I don't believe they do, they'll try to find you privately."

Emlyn had assumed that a museum in need of donations and visitors and gift shop sales would find publicity a terrific thing. But she could see the argument for silence.

"There were paintings stolen from a museum in Boston a few year ago," added Donovan, "and I remember the museum begging the thief to return them. Anything, we'll do anything, they said. We won't prosecute, we won't tell, we won't do anything, just don't hurt the paintings, and please give them back."

Emlyn thought of the mummy she had nearly dropped, the mummy from which something had fallen. Twice. The mummy would be easy to hurt. She thought of a museum staff whose entire purpose was to keep their stuff safe. Did they love Amaral-Re? Would they gather and weep and worry?

"Anyway," said Jack, "it's all of us. We agreed on that from the beginning. All five are doing it, all five are responsible."

"Besides," said Donovan, "it's a senior prank. It's not theft. We're just borrowing it in a very dramatic way."

Emlyn swiveled in her seat to make sure Donovan wasn't touching the mummy. Her family's car did not have swivel seats. She must suggest this kind of vehicle to her father.

"Drive faster, will you?" grumbled Donovan.

"Can't. I've had three speeding tickets. I've got points against my driver's license. I get another speeding ticket and guess how long I lose my license for?"

"How long?"

"A year."

A year meant nothing to Emlyn. She rarely drove. It could be a year before she got to drive again anyway.

"You're sure your grandparents' cottage is the place to keep the mummy?" she said to Donovan. They had been over this twenty times. But she needed to hear it again.

"They haven't closed the cottage for the season. They'll be back. But I promise you, they don't go up to the loft. They can't get up the ladder anymore, it's vertical, and the rungs are far apart and don't have much toe space, and my grandparents can't climb. They can hardly even get up out of their chairs. So we put the mummy up under my bunk bed. It'll keep just fine."

Emlyn's grandparents also had a cottage on a lake. They didn't own it. Every year they rented the same little bungalow for the same two weeks. They reclined on the same lawn chairs and waded in the same water. Emlyn had gone with them a few times. It was pretty quiet. You had to bring a lot of books.

Her other set of grandparents had taken up world travel. They preferred low-end tours with as many elderly people as possible crammed onto a bus. They started Europe from the south up, because they wanted to be warm. Over and over they went to Sicily in July and Italy in August. They were warm enough. They took thousands of photographs, and Emlyn was the only person on earth willing to look at these.

At Christmas, they took roll after roll of film of their three grandchildren. They couldn't get enough photographs of Emlyn.

She had a grotesque vision of other photographs of herself. Police photographs. And what would her grandparents feel about her then?

Jack left the interstate. It was a traveler's exit with three gas stations, pancake house, hamburger place, tacos, doughnuts. They stopped and everybody went to the bathroom and then got a hamburger. In the bathroom Emlyn wrapped her remaining gloves in paper towels and crushed them up and dropped them in the trash.

By now the museum staff would have found the glove that was keeping the basement door open. She imagined them saving it for the police. She imagined them standing in the Egyptian Room by the empty bier. The shock. The disbelief.

She was feeling shock and disbelief herself.

Eight more miles brought them to a small lake that gleamed in the moonlight. It was surrounded with tiny houses so close to one another they were like tents in an army camp. Each had a tiny unpaved driveway, towering trees, and a strip of garden and gate. Each had two little steps in front and a little screened porch in back, hanging over the water. Tiny docks stuck out into the lake, narrow as ladders.

It was very quiet.

Donovan hopped out of the van and fiddled around with the light fixture on the teeny front stoop.

"You open the door by turning a lightbulb?" said Jack.

Donovan laughed. "I don't have a key. But they keep one hanging inside the lamp. So does everybody else around the lake. Just a little tip, in case you want to make off with somebody's twenty-year-old black-and-white TV."

Inside the cottage was a darling little kitchen, like a toy, and a living room so small Emlyn

120

could not imagine having grandchildren visit on a rainy day. The ladder to the loft really was vertical. Emlyn and Donovan reached the top, and Jack handed them the mummy's feet, and they crouched while he fed the mummy upward.

The front of the loft had no wall, just a sort of curb. "What did you do when you were babies?" she asked Donovan. "Fall off and bounce?"

He laughed. "There used to be a gate. They took it down once we got older." He turned on the light in the loft.

There were three bunks, one against each wall. The ceiling was too low for a second bed above them. The floor had exactly enough space to lay Amaral-Re down.

They took the plastic off quickly, gently removing the masking tape from the mummy's shoulders and sides.

"Don't touch her," said Emlyn thickly. "We can't get oil or bacteria on her."

But it was impossible not to touch. They stroked her painted hair, black as night, and her lips, dark red. They felt her sharp elbows and ran their hands over the triangle of her captured feet.

"Wow," said Jack. "Three thousand years old. Wow."

"In the exhibit," said Donovan shakily, "it didn't seem so — well — fantastic."

"It seemed smaller," said Jack.

"Less important," said Donovan.

"Is that real gold?" whispered Jack.

"You know it is," said Donovan.

"Is it going to look amazing hanging up in that bell tower, or what?" said Jack.

"Don't call her *it*," said Emlyn. "She's a she. And we can't hang her in the bell tower."

"Oh," said Jack. "Where do you want to hang her, then?" He turned as if accepting her expertise on senior pranks.

"She's not sturdy and she might fall apart," said Emlyn. "And what if it rains? We can't let her get wet. It doesn't rain in Egypt."

The boys began to laugh.

"You're really taking this seriously," said Jack.

"Amaral-Re took her death very seriously."

"Well, yeah, but she's had time to get used to it, Em."

She knew she was not thinking clearly. The evening had truly taken everything out of her. This was how Amaral must have felt when her brains were removed by the embalmers. Emlyn had thought she would rejoice, would hug herself with the delight of her Bad, the success of her Wrong. But there was no such feeling. There was just a deep, appalling dread.

She had not known the mummy would be real.

Even though she had taken the mummy, lifted and hoisted and sweated to take this mummy, she had not known the mummy would be real.

"I'm exhausted," said Emlyn. "Let's get out of here. I feel as if I've rowed a hundred miles."

Jack looked at his watch. "Okay," he said with an unexpected reluctance. "I guess we can fit that in."

"Fit what in?" said Emlyn.

"It'll be on the news," said Jack. "Stolen mummies don't happen every day. Eleven P.M. is local news. I figured we'd stay here for the news, but

yeah, I think we can get to Lovell's just in time."
He gestured to Donovan, and the two of them
slid Amaral under a bunk, stowing her like old
sweatshirts.

Emlyn frowned. "Jack. You just said you didn't
think there would be publicity."

"Well — except, you know, the police report.
That part. That'll be in the news. So, hey, let's
go, you first, Em. I'm coming."

The ladder was harder to go down than it had
been to go up. From the floor she could not see
the bunks, let alone the mummy. Amaral was well
and truly hidden. But what if there was a fire?
What if —

Emlyn stared at Jack. He had a big, dumb grin
on his face. "You phoned the police, didn't you?
When we stopped for a hamburger, you called it
in on your car phone, didn't you? Because you
want publicity. You don't care what the museum
might want or what I might want."

"Aw, Em," said Jack, grinning, leaning down
toward her face as if the closer he got the more
she would agree. "It's no fun keeping secrets.
Gotta tell. I mean, they don't know it's us. They
don't know we took it. They don't know it has
anything to do with senior prank. All they know
is, a voice called and said there's been a theft
at the museum. A major artifact has been
stolen."

"You used those words? *Theft* and *stolen?*"

"Well, yeah. The police wouldn't come if I said
borrowed."

They walked out to the car. Donovan said,
"You really think that's real gold?"

Thirteen

Lovell lived in an apartment building several blocks east of Emlyn's, but everybody said "my house" even though nobody lived in a house. Way back in maybe second grade, Emlyn had been to a birthday party at Lovell's, because when they were littler everybody went to every party. They had never become friends. Just classmates who recognized each other.

Emlyn had no memory of the apartment although she could remember the little prize she had won. It had been a diary, its pencil attached by a gold ribbon. She had been so proud and had even written in it once.

It was only minutes before eleven when they pulled up at the apartment building.

In the lobby there was no doorman. Lovell could come and go much more anonymously than Emlyn. They pressed the buzzer, Lovell pressed back, they rushed in, stabbed the elevator button, and the boys all but hopped up and down to make the elevator lift more quickly.

"We've got the TV on," said Lovell, flinging open her door. "Quick! They've been giving teasers for the last half hour! 'Stay tuned,' they're crying, with those snarfy little smiles, 'for an exclusive story about the theft of a major work of art from the city museum!'"

Jack slapped his knee with joy. He and Maris hugged efficiently and separated and went straight to the TV. Then Maris said, "I am so impressed, Emlyn. I mean, really, in the end, I thought we'd all panic and run."

"She's not the panic-and-run type," said Lovell.

"She's awesome," said Jack. "But everybody stop talking. We don't want to miss a word."

Emlyn might not even have seen the TV, which was draped with plush, long-legged purple-and-violet creatures of unknown species. The apartment looked like a gift shop for creatures made of fur or velvet, corduroy and lace. Stuffed animals sat in rows on the couch and the chairs; they leaned on shelves and tipped in corners. There were pandas and lambs, camels and cats. There was no place to sit, unless you perched on the very rim of a sofa occupied by various teddy bear families.

"Mom and Vanessa and I collect stuffed animals," explained Lovell.

Lovell's father had left long ago. Possibly there had not been room for him. In any event, both mother and sister had dates tonight and were not back yet. Lovell didn't expect them before midnight. So they had an hour to talk things over in safety.

Everybody sat on the floor. Even the floor pillows were shaped like animals. Lovell handed Emlyn an immense, swollen pillow that turned out to be a pig with Velcro-attached piglets.

"You don't have to take the piglets off," said Lovell generously, "although, of course *we* never squash the piglets."

And they say the ancient Egyptians were weird, thought Emlyn.

She was aching all over. Every muscle felt strained and sickish. She had just been wondering if she was about to come down with the flu when she realized that the aches were from lifting a mummy over her head and running around with it. That would be an interesting reason to give the sports doctor.

She felt loose and unraveled, like the edges of Amaral's outer bandages.

Lovell and Maris had known about the television. Had publicity been part of the plan all along? What kind of team was this, anyway?

But I knew from the beginning, she thought. We weren't a team.

"We're going to be on television," sang Maris. She had a lovely voice, and Lovell joined her, a third lower, so they were a duet. "We're going to be on television," they sang together.

The four who were a team beamed at one another and put their arms around one another and rocked a little bit. Emlyn sat slightly behind them, her back supported against the teddy-occupied couch.

She felt dry and sick. Was the mummy really all right where they had left her? Donovan had implied that everybody around the entire lake kept keys hanging inside light fixtures, and if you needed a toaster or an old TV you could just walk in and take it. What would stop somebody from climbing that ladder and inspecting the loft? What would stop them from peering under that bunk?

Sensible robbers are after ATM machines, she told herself. Breaking into shiny new four-thousand-square-foot houses with landscaping. They are not in shabby little summer communities, climbing vertical ladders and poking in corners that can't have anything better than old beach towels.

Lovell's hostess technique was to lower bags of chips, tubs of sour cream, handfuls of chocolate bars, and boxes of cookies and doughnuts onto the floor. She tossed down some paper napkins and plastic cups and opened a huge plastic bottle of ginger ale. People who wanted ice struggled to their feet and ran to the freezer.

Emlyn just drank hers warm. She read the bag labels and settled on honey mustard pretzel bits. This would not have passed for dinner at her own household. Then she remembered that not only had everybody else had dinner, she herself had had a hamburger.

"Quiet, quiet!" yelled Donovan. "Here it comes! We're on!"

"Good evening!" said the anchor. As always,

she addressed her fellow newscaster instead of the actual audience. "James!" she cried. "Tell us about the dreadful, mysterious event at the museum!"

"Well, JoAnne," said James joyfully, "this evening, while the museum was occupied by more than seventy-five people at a fund-raising party and while guards were patrolling both inside and out, a very daring theft took place."

"That's you, Emmy!" shrieked Maris, spilling Cheez-Its on the carpet. She ate them anyway.

"Rhonda," cried James, "over to you!"

Rhonda, excited and laughing, was at the museum, standing by the pedestal on which the mummy had rested. "Forget Washington," said Rhonda happily, microphone against her mouth, notebook in hand, "forget scandal, forget Wall Street. We have something in our city immensely more surprising and interesting. The only mummy in the museum collection *has been stolen.*"

Rhonda certainly did not regard this as a crime. Rhonda regarded this as a cool, neat event. Thank you, grave robber, was Rhonda's approach.

"The mummy was taken sometime between eight and nine, when the museum theater was in use for a private party. The guard had just walked through the Egyptian Room. Dr. Brisband, director of the museum, was in his own office, hard at work. The thief is presumed to have entered and exited through the basement, where a door was found propped open with a black knit glove. With us tonight is Dr. Harris Brisband. Dr. Brisband, please tell us about the mummy. What is it worth? What are these thieves going to do with it?"

Gone was the distinguished urbane gentleman with his clever remarks, his jaunty bow tie, and his audience appeal. In front of the camera stood a horrified, heartsick, middle-aged man. His hair had tracks where he had been running his fingers through it. He definitely looked like a man coming down with the flu.

"I'm terribly shocked by this," he said. His voice trembled. He *was* shocked. "The mummy is one of our prized possessions. She is presumed by some of the hieroglyphs on her linens to have been royalty, but her connections have never been precisely established. However, the extraordinary care with which she was wrapped would indicate —"

"But what is this mummy worth?" interrupted Rhonda.

"It is not possible to put a dollar value on the mummy. The mummy cannot be replaced." He turned to the camera, leaving Rhonda on her own. "I beg of you," said Dr. Brisband, and he *was* begging, his face was ashen, "do not damage the mummy. She is very fragile. She *must* be kept flat. She cannot be —"

Emlyn had not kept Aramal-Re flat, even after the second time something fell or broke. He is begging *me*, thought Emlyn. He is looking into that camera, praying that *I* am watching and listening.

The realness of having taken the mummy was even more horrifying. She could not reassure Dr. Brisband that Amaral-Re was fine. Nor that she would be kept flat. Bell tower hangings were not gentle activities.

Rhonda broke in. "Dr. Brisband, we have spoken with the insurance company that covers the museum. They could not give us a dollar value, but you certainly can. What is that dollar value of that stolen mummy?"

All around Emlyn was the crunching of chips. Eyes were glued to the screen and hands moved blindly toward the sour cream and dipped messily. Soda was slurped.

"Dollar value?" whispered Lovell. "I never thought of that! Like, we could get a ransom!"

"Is it true," said Rhonda, "that you had CAT scans and X rays done on that very mummy only a few weeks ago? Is it true that those X rays proved that the mummy is hung with gold and precious gems, hidden by the linen wrappings all those thousands of years?"

"Oh, wow," breathed Jack. "Gold!"

"It's gotta be true," said Donovan. "Because that was definitely gold on her mask!"

It is true, thought Emlyn. I felt the gold in my heart when I held her.

Dr. Brisband said wearily, "A radiologist has examined the mummy. The X rays show solid material where one might expect a female Egyptian to have worn amulets, bracelets, anklets, and so on. But an X ray cannot distinguish between gold and tin or between gold and copper. Nobody knows whether the mummy is adorned with gold. Nobody will ever know."

"But if you believe she is a princess," said Rhonda, "you surely believe a princess would have been buried in real jewels. She would need them for her afterlife."

Dr. Brisband ignored Rhonda. He said to the camera, "The integrity of the mummy is what matters, not a few amulets we will never see. The mummy can so easily be destroyed. It is imperative that — "

"Now why," said Rhonda, as fiercely as if Dr. Brisband spent his time bilking innocent old couples of their retirement money, "was the thief able to pry open the case? Why weren't there alarms?"

Dr. Brisband looked exhausted. "Clearly, that was my error. I should have — "

"How do you expect to locate the mummy, Dr. Brisband? The police are still searching for clues, aren't they?"

"The integrity of the mummy," said Dr. Brisband, "precludes — "

"Listen to the jerk," said Maris. " 'The integrity of the mummy.' Come on. Why can't he talk like a normal person?"

The integrity of this mummy, thought Emlyn, is my responsibility. I'm the one whose plan was *not* to have integrity.

Rhonda was wearing that little frown reporters had when somebody back at the studio was giving orders through an earphone. She erased her frown, gave a shiny smile to the camera, and cried, "And this is live at the museum, where the city's only mummy has just been stolen. Back to you, JoAnne!"

JoAnne tried to be serious but failed. "James," she said, thoroughly enjoying herself, "neither the

131

police nor the insurance company will comment further, so we are left to speculate. *Why* was the mummy stolen? *Will* it be returned safely? *Are* there real gems and valuable gold beneath those frayed linen wrappings?"

They were no longer announcing facts. They were announcing that the mummy had a lot more value than being a mummy. If anybody thought they had only taken some bones wrapped in linen, they knew better now.

Jack had guessed right. The museum didn't want publicity. Well, thanks to Jack and the stupid TV crew, Dr. Brisband had publicity now.

And try as she might to remember the integrity of the mummy, Emlyn could not help wondering what the rattles inside Amaral-Re had been. A magnificent ring sliding off her finger? A ruby or topaz falling from her necklace? What if Amaral-Re really was adorned with treasure? Tutankhamen's tomb-type treasure? What if, only an inch or two down inside that linen, was a fortune?

Suddenly JoAnne and James were almost hopping out of their chairs. Gloating, JoAnne giggling out loud, they announced that their network, and their network alone had found the radiologist who had taken the X rays.

In a moment, the X ray was in front of the camera for the world to see. It was definitely Amaral-Re. The elbows stuck out at the sides, just where they had poked into Emlyn. The film showed a remarkable amount of jewelry.

A necklace extended from the mummy's shoulders halfway down her chest. It appeared to be a row of tiny dolls, and the radiologist explained that these were amulets, to keep her safe.

"Well, if they had value," snickered James, "it's in the gold, because those amulets sure didn't keep that girl safe."

"Oh, my god!" whispered Maris over and over. "Look, look, look!"

At the mummy's waist was a beltlike curve, dripping with more solid things. One arm must have had twenty bangle bracelets, going from wrist to elbow, and twenty more from elbow to shoulder. The other arm, above the elbow, wore a large band. All ten fingers had solid tips, as did all ten toes.

"What's on her fingers and toes?" JoAnne asked the radiologist. "They don't seem to be rings."

"Those are finger caps. Gold cylinders to keep the fingernails from falling off when the mummy's flesh dries out."

"Oooooh, that's sick," said JoAnne, loving it. "So you are saying that it's definitely gold?"

"Well, no, you can't identify a metal in an X ray. But when unwrapped mummies are found with finger and toe caps, they usually are gold."

"And so the thieves — " said James.

"Thieves!" said the radiologist. "They're grave robbers. They're no better than the scum of ancient days who ripped open tombs. The integrity of — "

"Here we go again," said Lovell.

"Grave robbers," said Jack. "I love it. That'll be our secret nickname."

As if Jack believed in secrets.

And then, sorrowfully, JoAnne and James had to discuss a school board meeting, in which it had been determined . . .

Jack, in possession of the remote, clicked JoAnne and James away, and they vanished into their dark screen like mummies into tombs. "Yea, Grave Robbers!" he yelled.

"Wow," said Maris, totally content. "We got everything. We got the mummy, we got the publicity, we got extra publicity because our mummy is extra, extra special. Emlyn, you are a wizard."

"Tell us every single detail, Emlyn," said Lovell. "Don't leave anything out."

"And don't pretend you weren't scared," said Maris, "because you had to have been scared. So include the scary parts."

Emlyn felt as if they were trying to unwrap her. Trying to rip off her outsides and reach into her belly for her gold.

What did happen at that museum? she wondered. I am different. Amaral-Re is certainly different.

"Come on, Emmy," said Donovan, nudging her. "Start with when you're alone in the office. It's dark. You have hours to wait. Start with that."

Emlyn said, "It was straightforward. The only problem was that the door I thought I could get out of I couldn't get out of. I took the freight elevator into the cellar and went out that way."

They sat staring.

"Emlyn," said Maris. "That's not fair. We want to know. It can't have been that simple. Donovan said on the phone from the car that you were terrified and sweating and running and falling."

They would interrogate her all night. She remembered to her dismay that she was spending all night here. It would be torture. The last thing she wanted was to be near Lovell hour after hour. Nobody had sparc bedrooms — she'd be in Lovell's room. Maris might stay over, too.

"Donovan exaggerates," said Emlyn. "Now. Let's talk about getting the mummy up to the bell tower."

For a moment, she didn't think they would let it go.

But eventually Donovan said, "I was thinking that we should just go in broad daylight. Barge right in and don't make any secret of what we've got and what we're doing."

"It's just like the muscum, in a way," said Maris. "We used the old mansion to get into the new museum, and now we're going to use the new high school to get into the old bell tower. There's a nice symmetry there."

"You mean, walk right through the guidance offices holding the mummy in the air while the guidance counselors are sitting there? So they know who took it?" demanded Emlyn.

"Of course, he doesn't mean that," said Jack. "We'll decoy them away, that's a cinch. Then we'll go in."

"During the day?" said Emlyn. "No, we won't!"

"Okay, we won't," said Maris quickly.

They were treating her like the team captain. She relaxed a little.

"The thing that worries me is," said Jack,

"they'll take the mummy down as soon as we get it up. The minute the administration sees it there, they're going to call the museum and the cops. So what we'll do is, we'll pour superglue into the bell tower lock once we leave. They'll have to erect scaffolding to get up to the mummy."

"No superglue," said Emlyn. "That's vandalism. They'd have to drill out the whole lock to replace it, and I don't want us to — "

They were all laughing. "Emlyn," said Maris, spilling soda on Lovell's carpet. Lovell just laughed and mopped with a paper napkin. "You who steal from museums are worried about putting glue in a lock?"

"I'm worried about everything."

Lovell cleaned the carpet. Maris folded up the chip bags. Jack stacked paper cups.

Donovan said, "You're right, Emlyn. We're just being silly because we're so excited. We don't want trouble, either. Tell you what," he said. "Since the cottage will still be empty tomorrow and we don't have school, how about we have a mummy party? Just the five of us? Can you get the van again, Jack?"

"Yes!" cried Lovell. "A real party, because we really have something to celebrate. And because Maris and I haven't seen the mummy yet."

"We've hardly seen the mummy, either," said Donovan. "Emlyn really hustled us out of there."

"We'll want mummy food," said Maris. "Mummy drinks. Mummy favors."

"And we'll dress like mummies," said Lovell.

"Cut it out," said Jack. "I'm all for a party, but let's have regular food. I saw a grill. Let's have hamburgers. And I'm not dressing like a mummy. I'm dressing like me."

"Hot dogs," said Donovan.

"Both," said Jack.

"The party will really be for you, Emmy," said Maris. "To celebrate you and your guts. We'll have a toast to ancient Egypt, and then we'll figure out how we get that thing into the bell tower without getting caught there, either. You must have a plan, Em, we know you. You're ready."

Fourteen

The next morning, Emlyn phoned her parents at work to tell them about the lake party. How pleased they were! Parents were always glad to see signs that you were popular. They didn't mind at all if the barbecue didn't start till late because Jack couldn't get the van until five.

It was a lovely day, one of those autumn days in which the colors were intense and the wind high, but there was no chill: It was summer saying good-bye.

The water glimmered. When the sun set, the breeze came up, and sweatshirts were piled on. Between the cottage and the lake was an old brick outdoor fireplace. Donovan made a huge fire, and when it had fallen to white-hot coals, they roasted their hot dogs and their hamburgers and ate standing up and laughing.

Maris had constructed marshmallow mummies with toothpicks. Using food coloring, she had painted tiny Egyptian symbols. Then she actually sliced a sheet of phyllo dough into tiny food bandages and wrapped the marshmallows into mummies.

Everybody had worn white after all. White sweatshirts or gray sweatshirts turned inside out and white pants or sweats.

Maris had an old tape of her mother's, "Walk Like an Egyptian." The five of them danced separately, not as if they were boys and girls and not as if two of them dated. Not even as if they knew one another. They danced as Emlyn thought ancient people must have danced, every movement between the dancers and their god.

Finally, when the coals were almost dead, they toasted their marshmallow mummies golden brown and oozing burnt sugar and sat on the long rim of the narrow deck with their bare toes in the cold water, chewing mummies.

"I've been thinking," said Lovell.

How different Lovell's voice suddenly was.

How careful.

And how careful Donovan and Jack and Maris seemed to be, also, their posture changed from a moment ago.

The slanting shadows of purple and black turned cruel and vengeful. The soft fleece of the inside of Emlyn's sweatshirt, which had made her feel safe and loved, lifted from her skin and left her cold and uncertain.

"Nobody knows," said Lovell very softly, "that we have the mummy."

"Nobody suspects," said Maris. "It is ten o'clock on Monday night, more than twenty-four hours after Amaral-Re was removed from the museum by Emlyn. They don't know. They don't have a clue. Nobody but us has the slightest idea in all the world that we are the owners of Amaral-Re."

"Every good party," said Lovell, "requires party favors. And our party favors are inside the cottage. Already wrapped."

"It would be so exciting," said Maris, "here at our mummy party, with our own mummy, to find out if there really is gold."

Emlyn's bare toes turned to ice in the water. The cold moved up her ankles and spread into her legs. She could feel it attack her spine and crawl into her heart.

"Mummy gold," breathed Maris.

"All we have to do," whispered Lovell, "is unwrap the mummy."

The water lapped softly, as lakes do, whispering around their edges, checking on their rocks, murmuring to their sand.

"No," said Emlyn loudly. "We cannot unwrap Amaral-Re. First of all, we're not the owners of the mummy. The museum is. That was our agreement. We will give her back. Second of all, mummies don't unwrap. The sap is dribbled over every layer. The linen solidifies like plaster. You'd have to use a saw."

The moon climbed a bit. It was not quite full. It had the awkward, sinister look of a failed circle.

"I have a saw," said Donovan. "It's in the shed. My grandfather prunes trees with it."

"Stop this! We will not unwrap her. There are photographs in the books about those Victorian unwrapping parties. They ended up ripping off the legs and head because the bones stick to the linen, and by the time the party was over, there was just a pile of snapped joints and pieces of skull and torn bandages."

"And gold," said Lovell.

Everything was a ghost. The moon. The water reflecting it. The peeling white cottage.

"It doesn't matter if there is gold. It is the integrity of the mummy that matters. We cannot hurt the mummy."

"It's dead, Emlyn," said Lovell, in the comforting voice of a baby-sitter. "Nothing will hurt it."

"It might get damaged a little teeny bit," said Maris, "but the thing to remember is, just making a mummy damages it. They took out the brains, Emlyn. With a hook through the nose. They sliced the whole gut open and took out the liver and lungs. That's called damage. We're just doing a speck more a few centuries later."

"If it's gold," said Donovan, "and if it's precious gems, the fortune is ours."

Emlyn drew her feet out of the water. Now they were even colder as the wind wrapped around them and curled under them. "There isn't a fortune," said Emlyn. "A fortune would weight a lot. What showed up on that X ray is probably paper-thin."

Maris lost patience. She stopped murmuring

and began talking stridently, making her point with volume. "Three-thousand-year-old gold bracelets, armbands, and rings? In perfect condition? As fabulous as anything from the tomb of Tutankhamen? Sitting right in our hands? It would be worth a fortune whether it's gold or painted glass, Emlyn, and you know it."

"It is not sitting in our hands. It is part of Amaral. She cannot be ripped apart and plundered."

Donovan shrugged. "Come on, Emlyn. Her grave was plundered when they brought her here. We'll be following a fine old tradition."

Emlyn was hanging onto her breath, her brain, and her cold feet. I started this, she thought. Well, here it is. Bad. Bad all the way through. "What about the senior prank?"

"I think we've pretty much lost interest in senior pranks," said Lovell. "Let those other guys put a cow up there. We have better things to think about."

"Gold," said Maris. "And diamonds."

"You're making up that part about the diamonds," said Emlyn. "You don't even know if they had diamonds in ancient Egypt."

They were sitting on a row along the dock. Maris and Lovell were staring down into the water, and their long hair shielded their faces from Emlyn's sight. Donovan was lying down on his back, feet in the water, eyes on the moon. Jack was leaning way back, supporting himself with his hands spread behind him. Emlyn could not see him at all because he was last in line.

She said, "Suppose we did saw into the

mummy and take out this jewelry. What are we going to do with it? It's not as if we can walk into high school wearing the necklace over a T-shirt. People are going to know we didn't get it at the mall. And even if most kids think it's cool that we're the grave robbers, there's going to be some kid who won't think so. There's going to be some kid who will phone the police. So we can't wear this. And you can hardly take an authentic three-thousand-year-old Egyptian amulet into some jewelry store and ask them to give you a million dollars for it. They've seen the news, too. They'll know perfectly well where it came from. The police would be there in five minutes. And if you decide to melt the gold down, you won't have anything. Because the value would be in the thing itself: the actual real jewelry of an actual real Egyptian princess."

"Right," said Maris.

Emlyn sagged in relief. She had converted Maris, then, who was the tough one. She didn't believe the boys cared about the jewelry.

"So what we do," said Maris, "is split the gold up. A few years from now, when we're in other states at various colleges or we've gotten jobs somewhere, we'll sell it. We'll be rich. There's going to be diamonds in there, and rubies, and pearls, and emeralds. And gold. A whole lot of gold."

Emlyn could hardly move her lips. "I read a lot about mummies," she said. "Nobody mentioned diamonds or rubies or pearls or emeralds."

"Gold, though?" asked Donovan. "They mention gold?"

143

"No matter when we sell, though," said Jack, "and no matter where, it will be recognized."

"How?" said Lovell. "Nobody has ever seen it."

This was true.

Nobody could identify it. Nobody had seen this jewelry since Amaral's family put it on her. "No!" said Emlyn. "She's real. She is a real thing, and she was a real person, and she deserves to stay herself. We cannot do this."

"I vote we unwrap the mummy," said Lovell.

"Yes," said Maris.

"Yes," said Donovan.

They had greed, the way ancient tomb robbers had greed, the way the reporters had greed. Grave robbers were greedy for gold and reporters greedy for scandal, but it came to the same thing. What can we destroy in order to get money or attention?

I who fell into a daydream and felt Amaral's heavy braids and soft sandals, I will have destroyed her. If it were not for me, she would have had her immortality, even if it was in a museum display. But I will be the instrument that ends her.

She imagined the saw, its sharp triangles ripping through the chest of a girl who had waited for thirty centuries to be resurrected. She heard the hideous tear, like open-heart surgery. Maris would tuck her fingers into the slit of the chest cavity and rip backward and open the mummy to the air. Maris's fingers would claw at jewels.

Amaral's eyes would continue to stare at the

144

heavens until they sawed off her face and grabbed for her skull to gather in the jewels adorning her real hair.

"I don't think we should," said Jack. He'd been wearing his sweatshirt like a cape over his shoulders, sleeves loosely overlapped to keep it on. He took it off and wrapped it around Emlyn. She needed the warmth. She appreciated the gesture. But was it a bribe? Whose side was he actually on?

"Oh, come on, Jack," said Maris. "How many people get to celebrate Halloween by actually cutting into a mummy?"

Jack said, "We don't any of us need money."

"Speak for yourself," said Donovan.

"Come on, Donovan. You work to pay for movies and clothes and CDs and candy bars. You don't work because you'd starve."

"If I had gold, I could have my own car."

"There's no place to park your own car in the city."

"Enough gold and I could rent garage space."

"You wouldn't be able to risk selling your share for years. All it's going to be is stuff to hide. We know how hard it is to hide things."

"It's hard to hide great big things, like mummies," said Maris. "It'll be a snap to hide little things, like gold diadems."

"No!" said Emlyn. "You touch that mummy and I call the police right now and tell them exactly where the mummy is and what we did."

"We?" said Maris. "Emlyn, I don't think *we* did anything. *You* are the thief here." Maris stood up slowly, looming over Emlyn.

How narrow the dock seemed. How deep and dark the water.

"You want to be fingerprinted, Emlyn? Put in a cell with druggies who ripped somebody's face open with a broken bottle? You want a cell with a hole instead of a toilet? You want your mother getting a phone call from the police? You want those reporters, that JoAnne and that James, all beaming and happy and pushing their microphone in your father's face? You want to be thrown out of school? You won't be allowed to finish your senior year, you know."

"Maris, give it a rest," said Jack sharply. "We're not going to attack Emlyn, okay?"

"Of course, we're not going to attack Emlyn," said Maris sweetly. "We're going to unwrap a mummy."

But it was Donovan who made the first move. He walked solidly and rhythmically up the dock to shore. The old wooden pier swayed beneath his pace and his weight. On the back corner of the tiny cottage was a small lean-to. Its padlock was for show because he just opened the door while the padlock hung off the hasp. He took something out. He came back down the dock.

Emlyn had pictured a saw blade several inches wide, a long rectangle, slanting to a narrower front end. But this was a shaped like a very large capital D, with the blade the straight line. The blade was an inch high and perhaps two feet long, with vicious teeth. The curve of the D was red metal, which Donovan gripped where the curve ran into the upright.

He grinned. It was no sloppy, friendly grin. He

shoved the saw into the air like an executioner with an ax. "The mummy," said Donovan, "awaits."

If it came to some sort of grappling — actual, real fighting, which made Emlyn physically ill — the thought of her fists and their fingernails — there would be a fragile mummy between them. Amaral would be smashed and ruined even if Donovan didn't cut into her.

"The metal kitchen table opens up," said Donovan. "It's this old-fashioned thing from when my grandmother was a girl. Plenty of room for a five-foot mummy. Be easy to clean afterward, like a surgical table."

"We won't hurt the table," Maris assured him.

"No, because we won't cut all the way through the mummy," agreed Donovan. "We'll cut through the plaster and when we hit jewels or bones, we stop. I promise not to sever any heads or hips, Emlyn." He was laughing. "And no matter how you complain, you get your fair share of gold. After all, you're the thief."

147

Fifteen

How strange to find that being caught in the museum would have been better. Emlyn would have been in trouble, yes; but it would have been *her* trouble. Not Amaral's trouble.

"Emlyn, you okay?" said Jack, as if puzzled.

"Of course, I'm not okay! This is terrible. Jack, please help me. Please be on my side."

Jack looked embarrassed. "Em, I can't really get into this."

"You *are* in it, Jack. We're all in it." She had no plans. She had no strategies. In fact, Emlyn did not seem to have much of a brain right now.

"No, you don't understand," said Jack. "I mean, I can't seem to work up a lot of interest. I wouldn't saw the mummy up on my own, but I'm not going to go to war to stop it, either."

Emlyn felt desperately tired. Her father's philosophy of life was that everything would look better in the morning. He often said to his three children, "Have a good night's rest. You'll know what to do when you get up."

But the advice did not apply. If she went off to get a good night's rest, in the morning there would no mummy. She must stay awake, and she must prevent this.

But she was afraid of the saw. She was afraid of Donovan, and his smile, and his tight grip on the saw handle. The blade was rusty. It was not sharp. He did not hold the saw with care but with greed. His strength was considerable. When he yanked on that blade he would go right through Amaral. He would slice her actual bones, her real chest.

"You know what, guys," said Jack. "Let's cool off. Literally. Let's go for a swim."

Okay, thought Emlyn. They swim. I run to the cottage, lift the mummy, leap like Superman from the loft! Speed to the van! And then they'll just get out of the water and stop me. And Jack has his keys. And if I get into the van with the mummy and lock the doors, he'll just press the remote on his key chain and open them again.

"You and Emlyn go for a swim, Jack," laughed Maris. "And when you get back," she said, singsong, "it'll be a whole different mummy."

Think swimming, Emlyn told herself. There's a skiff tied to the end of that neighbor's dock. I can row — but so what? First I'd have to get the mummy down here.

Donovan was headed back up the swaying dock, Maris and Lovell trotting after him, discussing the order in which the mummy's jewels should be divided. "You have an attitude, Emlyn," said Lovell. "You come last."

In a minute they would be groping in brittle bones, screaming with joy as they retrieved gold from a dead person.

One by one they left the dock, crossed a scrap of grass, climbed three sagging steps, and went through a torn screen door. The tiny screened porch had old, sagging wicker chairs and a huge geranium with scarlet blooms. You could slump there and retrieve yourself, and when you had pulled yourself together there would be a lake waiting. But Emlyn could not slump. And she could think of no way to retrieve this situation.

If I could get the mummy, she thought, *I'd give it back*. I got into that museum. *I can get into it again*.

Donovan and Lovell were already getting the mummy down from the loft, and Maris was fussing with something in the kitchen, and Jack had not yet gotten in the tiny door. Finally, he moved ahead, and Emlyn was inside.

It was minuscule. Truly a vacation kitchen, where meals were simple or cooked outdoors. You would keep no extra dishes here, no vase of flowers. If you made a pot of coffee and scrambled an egg, the whole kitchen would be used up.

There was no dining room, just a trio of windows in the living room that looked through the screened porch and across the lake. In front of these were the metal table and six sturdy wooden chairs that looked as if they had been purchased before Donovan's grandparents had been born.

She had noticed the telephone when they arrived. It was as old-fashioned as the rest of the place and still had a dial. Emlyn had hardly ever used a dial.

The phone was gone. They had taken her seriously. They were going to make sure she could not call the police. She had not brought her purse and did not have her cell phone or even her driver's license. What would she say if she could find a phone? If she did dial 911? "Hi. A friend of mine who's been dead thirty centuries is being threatened"?

Donovan ran his thumb along the evil teeth of the saw and cut himself.

How stupid he is, thought Emlyn, knowing that rust carried tetanus; knowing that most of the people in this room would have had their last booster shot when they were four or five.

"Don't get blood on the mummy," said Maris. She was laughing wildly. "After all, old Emlyn here is going to bag up the bones when we're done and carry them back to Dr. Brisband. They'll test the blood spots and get your DNA. So — "

"Forget it," said Lovell, "Emlyn is not carrying leftover bones anywhere. Once we have this gold, we can't let anybody know. Right now, we're still within reach of senior prank. We take the gold, and it's really theft and it's really us and we're all really doing it."

This did not slow anybody down. If anything, they were twice as excited.

"What are we going to do with the bones?" said Jack.

Donovan set down the saw, washed his cut, and put on a Band-Aid.

"Bury them in the backyard?" asked Maris.

"No," said Donovan, "divide the stuff into trash bags and drop them off in the wastebaskets at gas stations on the way home."

Oh, Amaral-Re! thought Emlyn. From a pyramid to a trash can at a truck stop. "We are not going through with this," she said.

"Yeah," said Jack. "Let's slow down. We have the mummy. We have time. There's no rush. The gold has waited centuries. It can wait longer."

"Not here, it can't, " said Donovan. "My grandparents come back this week. They're always here for fall foliage. Then they close the cottage. That means screwing big, flat boards over every window and door. I mean, we could still get in — a screwdriver is all it takes, and time. But still."

"But still," said Jack. "We want to stay friends and all. And it was Emlyn who did the real work. We just had the idea. I think she gets two votes. In fact, I'd say Emlyn gets the only vote."

Emlyn prayed this time. It was all right to ask God for help when you were doing a right thing. God, she said, thank you for putting Jack on my side.

"If you were voting, Jack," said Maris, "what would your vote be?"

An odd look passed between them. It meant a lot, but Emlyn could not read it. Was it affection? A message?

"I want to think about it," said Jack.

And then the whole thing changed. Lovell got

bored. She buttoned her jacket. "Listen, guys, we have school tomorrow, and I haven't done a lick of homework. It'll be late when we get home. We need to get going." She turned to Emlyn. "We were just wired, Emmy. We weren't going to do anything. Donovan, you shouldn't have gone and gotten the saw. It got us bent out of shape."

"And Donovan, get a tetanus shot," said Maris. "That was dumb, cutting yourself on a rusty tool."

Donovan nodded for a while. This time he ran the Band-Aid down the blade. He was more careful. No blood. He smiled at Emlyn. "We wouldn't really have done it, Em," said Donovan. It was a lovely smile. Completely charming.

"We were just kidding," said Maris. "You take everything too seriously, Em."

Jack pulled his car keys out of his pocket. "Let's roll then," he said. He stretched his arms and beat a tattoo on his chest. "What do you mean — a lick of homework?"

"My grandmother says that. A lick of housework, a lick of shopping."

"A lick of mummy-stealing," said Maris. "Come on, everybody got everything? Let's go."

They headed for the van.

Maris and Jack sat in front.

Lovell and Emlyn sat in the middle.

Donovan stretched out in the rear.

The mummy, thought Emlyn. We didn't put the mummy back in the loft. We left Amaral on the metal table. So we're coming back before Donovan's grandparents show up. That means

153

we have to get back here another school night. And not one person here but me can do that. Because every other person has practice or rehearsal or a job. And only Jack has transportation.

So . . .

Jack let the radio search, and little blips of rock and easy listening and talk scooted by as it hunted for good reception.

"Did we get punchy, or what?" said Maris. "Tomorrow we meet and figure out when and how we take the mummy up to the bell tower."

"Right. Skip second period?" said Jack.

"Deal," said Donovan.

"Done," said Lovell.

The return trip seemed to take forever. Nobody talked. Emlyn half slept.

Jack dropped Donovan off first and trucked on to Lovell's. Then he and Maris dropped Emlyn off. "Listen, Em," said Jack, "don't worry so much. We got carried away, but we're really stand-up guys. We aren't going to do anything but senior prank."

"It was the moonlight," said Maris. "We know how seriously you feel about your mummy."

"Okay," said Emlyn. "Thanks. And thanks for calming everybody down, Jack."

"Good night, then."

She walked into the lobby of her apartment building and turned to look back.

To get to Maris's, Jack needed to turn right at the corner.

But the van went straight.

Jack, she thought, Jack. Why did you give me your sweatshirt? Why did you take my side? Why did you cool everybody down? So that you and Maris could go back by yourselves and keep all the gold?

Or is this my usual nonsense, and you're really deeply in love, and you're going to park on some side street and make out, or go to some late-night restaurant and have a romantic meal by candle-light?

Emlyn got into the elevator. "Hey! How are ya?" said the elevator guy.

"Fine, thanks. How are you?"

He told her. He was a nice enough person but far too willing to tell you how he was. He was never well. Emlyn waited for him to discuss his digestion and his prescriptions, and finally he opened the doors for her and she went into her apartment.

Ten past midnight. The place was utterly quiet. They had left the light on over the piano, a soft, low light so she could see where to walk but wouldn't startle people who were falling asleep.

Her parents watched the eleven o'clock news sitting up in bed, and at eleven thirty they clicked it off, tipped over, and went to sleep. They were like windup dolls, hitting the end of the day. The boys were so energetic they couldn't make it past nine, and they slept as soundly as Amaral.

Still, she tiptoed as if somebody might appear.

On the high, narrow table where they kept mail and to-do lists and permission slips for the boys lay the car keys in a little key pile.

Emlyn slid into her room and changed into

155

dark clothing. Then she took the car keys and ran down the seven flights of stairs to the ground floor, and one more flight to the silent garage below.

Her parents' Ford wagon had been pretty beat up when they bought it. Years in the city had given it dents and scratches and dulled the finish. It looked exactly like what it was: a tough old box with wheels.

Emlyn started the car and drove in the scary half dark to the exit. When she clicked her visor control, high, thin steel rods slid back into the floor so she could drive out.

She checked the gas gauge. Plenty.

Emlyn rarely drove. They didn't use the car that much, and when they did, her parents always insisted there was too much traffic for Emlyn to be at the wheel. Well, midnight on Monday, there was not too much traffic. There wasn't even another car. She was glad to make it to the interstate where there was always traffic. Trucks whipped past like monsters, their drivers too high to be visible.

Exit 65, she thought, and decided she could drive as fast as the trucks, so she did. Exit 65 came right up. The gas station was still open and the doughnut place, but not the other restaurants. She turned on the country road to go the eight miles to the lake.

She was worried about finding the right cottage. There had been so many of them, all painted white, all with dark shutters and the same tiny docks out into the lake.

She hadn't been paying enough attention on

either trip. The driver always knew more than the passenger. What had happened to the Emlyn who prided herself on being so observant that, if anybody ever needed a witness to testify, she would be the one who really knew what was going on? Perhaps there had never been such an Emlyn.

Her fingers gripped the steering wheel too tightly. She couldn't find anything on the radio she could bear to listen to.

Finding the cottage was easier than she had expected.

Jack's van was parked in the little front yard.

Sixteen

It was one thirty in the morning. The moon drifted in and out of purple clouds. The lake was alive with shifting shadow.

Even the third week in October was too late in the year for most people to live in an unheated summer cottage. None of the tiny houses looked occupied. But even in summer, one thirty Monday morning was not an hour when people would be driving around. So any car slowly cruising down this road at this hour was going to be of interest to Jack and whoever was with him.

Who *was* with him?

Had Jack and Maris simply turned around after they deposited Emlyn and picked up Donovan and Lovell again? How much of a team were those four? Did they know one another well enough to pass hand or eye signals? Had they silently agreed to get rid of prissy Emlyn? Or had she been so absorbed by her thoughts that they had been able to whisper back and forth, coming to a decision without her knowledge?

At this very moment, were the four of them sawing through the mummy?

Emlyn drove past the cottage. The little road was so narrow that it felt one way, but it wasn't. In the summer when there was traffic, cars must pull to the side in order to inch past one another. She would be afraid of scraping somebody's door handle off. Now, in the leaping, changing shadows as the moon and the clouds argued in the sky, the trees and bushes leaned down into the space she needed for driving and tried to cut her off.

Would Jack have the nerve to come without Donovan? she wondered. Even though we saw how easy it is to get in, would Jack dare to go in without Donovan?

She was being ridiculous; she had dared enter a huge public institution without permission. Why would Jack worry about entering one little cabin without permission?

She passed a number of tiny houses and a lot of tall trees, and then she turned off her headlights so she and her car would vanish into the dark. The scattered moonlight showed enough road for her to keep going.

What if Donovan was loping after her car right now? Reading the license plate? Ready to rip open her door?

Emlyn hit the lock button and heard the satisfying clicks of a car closing around her.

Stop this, she said to herself. You don't even know if Donovan's here, and even if he is, he isn't a murderer. He's just greedy. They're all greedy.

After about ten houses, the road looped inland, following the uneven shore of the little lake. Emlyn backed into a driveway so nobody could read her license plate, and she parked. In a normal neighborhood, ten houses would be quite a distance. Ten here were nothing; the houses were miniatures. She eased herself out of the wagon, shut the door as softly as she could, and locked it. Then she crossed the road and began to creep over the tiny yards toward the cottage.

There were many pines whose heavy branches offered solid protection, so she made her way from pine to pine. She tripped over a little row of lake stones that seemed to outline a garden. Her sneakers sank in the soft soil and crushed little stems.

Ahead of her sat the van, its darkened windows like holes in the night, blacker than the sky.

She had no plan. Plans depended on things happening the way you expected them to. She had never expected this.

Like a blindfold over her thoughts and eyes was the face of Amaral-Re, gold and gleaming and silent. Amaral-Re would not beg or plead. Even as she was torn to pieces, as if by a pack of mangy coyotes, she would make no protest when her dignity was literally ripped to shreds.

It had seemed to Emlyn that Jack really had been on her side. He wanted to wait and think it

160

through. But it could not be, for Jack was the one with the van. If the driver said, No, we're not driving back to the cottage a second time, nobody could have done anything about it.

So Jack was just as eager to unwrap the mummy as the others. he had simply taken a different approach in getting rid of Emlyn.

She sank to her knees on grass as cold as the grass under the maples when she told them she had a master key. How she had loved that word *master*! But it turned out that when things went wrong, they went completely wrong, and if there was one thing that Emlyn was not, she was not master of this new situation.

So now I know, thought Emlyn, that when a criminal is double-crossed, she can hardly complain to the authorities. She has to deal with it herself.

She imagined putting cement shoes on Jack and Maris, Lovell and Donovan, and sinking them into the middle of the lake. But at the same time, she imagined what they would find when they carved Amaral-Re open.

What *had* Amaral worn into death? What had her weeping parents put about her throat and fastened about her waist? What had they woven into her hair and hung from her ears? Would there be an amulet of the jackal god, Anubis? A crown of inlaid silver and a scarab of carnelian? Was it spectacularly magnificent jewelry? Ornate and intricate and staggeringly beautiful?

Or were those bracelets just circles of copper — cheap then, cheap now?

Emlyn though of the tired little card she had taken for a souvenir. Some souvenir. The others were getting a gold bracelet. Hammered into rosettes, perhaps, and set with turquoise. The others would have an actual belt of solid gold. Earrings pierced with precious stones, gleaming with ruby and sapphire and —

Stop it, Emlyn told herself. Whatever it is, it must lie with Amaral-Re forever. It must not be torn from her.

The front door of the cottage opened.

Emlyn was beneath the heavy branches of an immense pine, encircled by its little pine sisters and brothers.

Awkwardly, Jack held the door for Maris, and together they backed out of the door, easing their way down the two little steps. Between them, they held a large shiny black cylinder, like a very large, very heavy poster tube.

Emlyn closed her eyes and thanked God. Which God? she thought. Mine? Or Amaral's?

Amaral would have worshipped many gods. Beautiful, strange, terrifying gods with beautiful, strange, terrifying habits.

They were being very careful, considering what they planned to do with Amaral-Re in a little while. They handled her as if she were more precious than a new baby. They eased her onto the floor of the van like a wounded patient, tucking her carefully between the seats. Maris settled in the front passenger seat. Jack went back, locked the door, hung the key where it belonged, and then, oddly, he walked around the cottage and disappeared on the lake side.

Emlyn ceased to breathe. Was he searching? Had he heard something?

When Jack reappeared, he was carrying the pruning saw.

She almost laughed. She should have guessed that. People in cities did not need such a saw, so Jack didn't have one at home. He was taking Donovan's.

Emlyn could not safely conclude that Donovan and Lovell had no idea what was happening. It was entirely possible that they simply couldn't stay out later.

Emlyn had no idea what their parents would think, or how much checking there was, or how much worry. But she *could* safely conclude that the mummy had not been cut. They were taking the mummy and the saw to a better location. And what might that be?

A location with no grandparents arriving soon.

One Emlyn would not know about and could not interfere with.

And where they could leave a mummy safely until they had time to use the saw.

Every one of them had to be in school in the morning, and school began at five minutes before eight. It was going to be three A.M. before anybody could get home and climb into bed. Tomorrow Donovan worked, Maris had play practice, Lovell soccer, and so did Jack.

Emlyn was sure, based on the party earlier that afternoon, that these four would not just grab any old ten minutes, split the mummy in half, and rip out what they wanted. They would make an event of it. They would want several hours, and they would want pleasures to accompany them: music, food, time to laugh, and time to celebrate.

So she would bet that they were not, in fact, going to tear open this mummy until next weekend. And she would also bet that even if Donovan and Lovell did not at this instant know what Jack and Maris were doing, Jack and Maris would not leave them out. They were a team; they needed all their players; it wouldn't be fun with only half the team there.

But what fun it would be to outwit the outsider . . . Emlyn.

I haven't played the game very well, she thought. If I wanted to keep my team on my side, I should have shared with them, told them more, giggled with them, trembled with them, let them in on my adventure. I actually chose to be the outsider. I didn't let any of them be anything except escort or driver.

Saw in hand, Jack walked around the van to the driver's door. He stood for a moment, looking up the road where Emlyn had driven her station wagon ten minutes earlier. Maris said something Emlyn could not hear. Illuminated by the ceiling light of the van, Maris looked incredibly beautiful. Her hair had fallen dramatically around her, and the light above shadowed her face. She, too, seemed immortal in her beauty.

But Jack paid no attention to her. He leaned forward and set the saw between the two front seats. Then, leaving his door open, Jack walked down the lane toward where she had parked the Ford.

Emlyn felt sick.

All he'll find is an old car, the kind old people drive, she told herself. He won't know it's my car. In the suburbs, kids probably know one another's cars, and the cars everybody's parents drive as well. But we don't recognize one another's cars because we don't drive them enough. Nobody's ever picked me up at school in this car. I don't have the slightest idea what anybody's father or mother drives. Or if they drive at all.

So he can check the car out as much as he wants. It won't tell him anything.

But Jack walked slowly. He wasn't sure what he was anxious about. He paused in front of the third house, but the road had not yet curved, and Emlyn's car was out of sight.

He shrugged visibly, came back to the van, got in, and drove away. Emlyn moved from pine to pine, watching his taillights. Much too quickly, the bright red pair of lights disappeared. Emlyn reconstructed the little road in her mind. Would he have reached the main road that fast?

She frowned a little and then followed carefully, threading her way from pine to pine, unsure of her footing; unsure of her reasoning.

Then she laughed silently. Yes. Jack had parked and turned off the lights and was waiting to see if anybody followed him out. So he *had* heard the car come down the road at the wrong time in the wrong season, and he *had* wondered.

Who was he afraid of?

She was sure he did not suspect that she, Emlyn, was smart enough to have followed him. So was he worried about police? Neighbors? Donovan? The museum?

165

Or was it just the general simmering sick worry when you knew you were wrong; you were terribly wrong; and you were deeply, horribly afraid that somebody else knew?

She sat on the ground again. She had waited a long time in the museum, and she could wait here, too. She did not believe Jack could wait. It was not his personality. She placed a private bet that he would last five minutes.

She lost. He didn't last two minutes. He started up the van, drove off, and she even saw, through the yards and trees, his thoughtful turn signal as he headed onto the eight-mile stretch back to the interstate.

She ran back to the Ford. She'd catch up and follow at a distance; find out what this place was where they believed they could safely stash Amaral-Re.

Jack could not risk a speeding ticket, even at this hour. Maybe especially at this hour. Get stopped by the police in the middle of the night when you were not yet eighteen and it was entirely possible the police would ask him just what was that big plastic-wrapped object lying on the floor? She didn't think they would have the right to search the van, but the police certainly knew about the missing mummy.

If you're weren't thinking about mummies, a big long old trash bag would just be odd; but if you had been told to keep your eyes out for a missing mummy (what jokes must be going the rounds over this!), that bump at one end and the triangular rise at the other might well remind you of feet and head . . . and mummies.

So Jack would set his cruise control just below the speed limit.

Emlyn set hers just above it. Jack and Maris had a two-minute start.

This time she felt like listening to music. She turned on her favorite station and sang along as she drove.

When she saw the van she stayed back so that she was nothing but a pair of headlights in their rearview mirror. Assuming they were headed home, there was only one possible exit for them to use. She let a couple of semis get between herself and the van. She'd see just fine when they took the exit and would have plenty of time to take it herself.

She stopped singing. Her mind was clear.

Her task was obvious.

To prevent its ruin, she must get the mummy back.

No matter what Jack and Maris thought, there was only one place on earth where the mummy was safe: back inside the museum.

The drive between the lake and the city was a little more than an hour, and Emlyn promised herself that by the time Jack took the downtown exit, she would know how she was going to get Amaral back into the museum.

Think doors, think windows, think utility courtyard, truck — hey.

I could ship Amaral back to the museum. Enough styrofoam peanuts and I can have her delivered —

Well, not quite.

Delivery required payment, addresses, a phone number . . .

Maybe she would deliver Amaral herself, in the night, setting her on the doorstep and calling the police or Dr. Brisband from her car. Yes, that was wiser. Forget the getting in and out. Forget packing and shipping. Set her down, run, and call. Get a weather report first, so it wasn't raining. A few things like that — but keep it simple.

She was planning so hard she forgot Jack, and it was with a shock that she glanced over and saw he had taken the exit. Her own car was flying past it; she hardly had time to get on the exit ramp, didn't have time to signal.

It was so much harder to do things than she had anticipated. Too many directions for thoughts to fly, and when she herself was flying at seventy miles an hour, there was not just the danger of getting caught. There was also the danger of splatting on the pavement.

City driving was pretty straightforward. The blocks were rectangles and squares; the lights turned red and green at predictable intervals. By the turns Jack took, Emlyn knew they were going to Maris's apartment building. She wanted to get close but couldn't risk it, so she just moved over a block and drove parallel to the van, crossing the cross streets exactly when they did, but a block to the east. It was fun and it worked.

Emlyn did not waste time looking for a space but just double-parked. She left her blinkers on so that anybody glancing at the vehicle would expect her back momentarily. She jumped out and ran to Maris's, staying on the opposite side of the street and stooping behind all the parked cars. It was much easier than when she had done this carrying a mummy. Parked cars gave her a solid fence to hide behind. She stationed herself directly across from the van.

Jack, too, double-parked, and he and Maris both got out. There did not appear to be a doorman in the building. Maybe he went off at midnight, or maybe they didn't have one. Emlyn liked having a doorman.

Together, Jack and Maris carried their plastic bag. Maris opened the outside door and then the inside door, and Emlyn could only guess what happened after that.

A moment later, Jack came back and just sat in the van.

Emlyn hoped nobody would drive by and see her peering between the hoods of cars she did not own. What if Maris could look down from her apartment? What if the people on this side had insomnia, and stood on their balcony with a cup of coffee, and called the police about the female crawling around their Buick?

Five entire minutes passed.

Then Maris was back. No mummy.

She and Jack talked, Maris ran back inside, and Jack drove away.

So he was the keeper of the saw, and Maris was holding the mummy.

Emlyn went back to her car and drove home. She had never entered her own parking garage in her own building at night, by herself. It was scarier than the basement of the museum. She could not think of a reason why she should have the car at this hour — she, Emlyn, whose specialty was thinking of falsehoods and lies. Her mind was pudding and her heart racing, and although it must be physiologically impossible, her racing heart was blinding her.

She wanted no doorman, no elevator guy, no neighbor to pop up out of the shadows and grab her arm, recognizing her in the night, demanding to know where she had been and what she was doing and maybe even march her inside to be interrogated by her parents.

But, of course, that wouldn't happen. Nobody would question her. Nobody would report her. She had let her nerves gain control.

She let herself into the apartment. It was silent. Nobody had awakened and found her gone. Nobody had panicked and called the police.

She put the car keys down where her mother or father had set them earlier.

She lay awake in the silent dark of her bedroom, the hours creeping toward dawn, as she planned the second theft of the same mummy.

Seventeen

Emlyn was astonished when she woke up, because this proved that she had, in fact, slept.

She had not set her alarm.

She was horrified to see that it was nine in the morning. School had started an hour ago. Emlyn was never late. She was never sick, either, and never missed school. She jumped up and ran through the apartment, but everybody was gone.

Nobody would have looked in on her. When they didn't see her at breakfast, they'd assumed she got up early, which she did a lot, and was already at school. The library opened an hour ahead of classes, and Emlyn often did her homework in the morning instead of the night before.

She felt weirdly isolated from the four other people who lived in this place. They knew nothing of what she was doing or thinking or suffer-

171

ing. It should have been lovely to be home alone in the soft morning peace of the apartment. She rarely saw the sun at this angle in these rooms. But she felt a queer anguish, as if she were some trespassing stranger.

She wanted almost desperately to hug her parents and even embrace her little brothers. Then she pulled herself together, dressed in her usual blend of khaki pants, dark sweater, white shirt, collar barely showing. She fixed her hair, put on a little lipstick, and reviewed her next theft. There was no way to do this one except by demand.

She walked the long, sunny blocks to Maris's apartment.

Maris would have gone to school no matter how tired she was and no matter how much she wanted to examine the mummy. If you hadn't been in school that day, you weren't allowed to go to any athletic practice or drama rehearsal. The rule was that if you weren't well enough to go to class, you weren't well enough to go to rehearsal. Maris had a lead; she would never skip rehearsal. She'd sleep through classes and fail quizzes instead.

Maris's mother worked at home. She was a consultant for something, Emlyn couldn't remember what. Her entire life was phone and fax. They had a million phone lines at Maris's, and you weren't supposed to use any of them.

Emlyn took the elevator up, knocked on the apartment door, and Maris's mother opened it. "Why, Emlyn," she said, confused. "Whatever are you doing here? Come right in, darling. Are you all right? Isn't this a school day? What day is this, anyhow?"

"No, you're right, it's Tuesday. Don't panic. I'm so sorry to bother you at work, I won't be here a second. It's just that Maris is storing a huge art project for me, and I got my times wrong, and I have to get it to art class right now. It's about five feet tall. It's very fragile. Papier-mâché. It's a person, see, and I didn't have five feet of space in my apartment, so Maris volunteered."

"Well, darling," said Maris's mother, even more puzzled. "There's no place here, either. Maris has put it under her bed or else it's hanging from the ceiling. Those are the choices. Our rule is, you buy something, you throw something else out. Otherwise we'd have to walk on top of our belongings. Let's go look. I'm skeptical, darling. If there was space for five feet of anything, I'd have filled it."

Maris's room was extremely small and extremely crowded, with built-ins and cubbies and hooks and possessions overflowing and tipping and jammed and doubled up.

Hanging by bungee cords from a ceiling hook, like a big, dead, vertical plant, were the taped-together trash bags. The chair Maris had stood on to hang it there was still right beneath the mummy. It looked like a suicide.

"I'm so lucky you're home," cried Emlyn, hopping up on the chair seat. She managed to balance the mummy and free the bungee cords. She

173

was amazed that the plaster had held. She would have expected the weight of the mummy to pull the whole ceiling down.

"I'm so glad I'm not an art teacher." Maris's mother shuddered. "What a mess it must be! Thirty teenagers making five-foot-tall papier-mâché dolls? How much papier-mâché is that? How much spilled goop?"

Emlyn threaded herself and her five-foot burden around the corner and toward the door. "My mother feels just the same. There's nothing messier."

"Do you need help?" asked Maris's mother, pushing the elevator button for her. "Shall I go down to the car for you?"

"Oh, no, thanks, papier-mâché hardly weighs a thing," said Emlyn, who had in fact blistered her shoulder from the friction of the mummy when she ran with it and was trying not to show the pain as the mummy now tore the blister open again. "Thank you so, so, so much. 'Bye now!"

She and Amaral rode the elevator down and left the lobby. Then she walked out into the daylight with a mummy in her arms.

In midmorning it was easy to flag a taxi. "Whatcha got?" said the driver. He was used to people carrying things around: porch chairs, long ceiling light tubes, baby carriages, Christmas trees. He helped her balance her package on the top of the front seat, sticking backward into the cab. Emlyn slid in back with the mummy's feet and gave him her address. "It's an art project for school. We made papier-mâché dolls."

"Oh, yeah? The kind at kids' parties? Where

they whack 'em open with baseball bats and grab the prizes?"

"Exactly," said Emlyn.

"Room for a lot of prizes in a doll that big," said the taxi driver. "What's the exact name? There's a special name."

Mummy, thought Emlyn, but she said, "Piñata."

"Piñata," repeated the taxi driver happily, and he dropped her off.

She repeated the piñata story to a resident of her building, to the doorman, the mailman, another neighbor, and finally, the elevator man. "Don't you have school?" they all said, frowning.

Cities were supposed to be anonymous. What was this small-town character this one had suddenly developed? She was sick of their interest in her life. "School," she agreed, smiling pleasantly. "It starts late for me today."

"Oh," they said, as if this were a sensible answer.

She got into the apartment without breaking her shoulder or her mummy. She put the mummy on her bed and peeled back the trash bags.

Amaral-Re was untouched. Her painted eyes still watched the ceiling, and her linens were tightly bound.

The bandages had been wrapped with astonishing care: woven basket-style, their pattern formed little squares surrounded by larger squares, like picture frames with many mats. Somebody had loved Amaral-Re. Somebody cared how she looked for eternity. Once she would have had a coffin, perhaps carved of cedar and shaped like the girl herself, adorned with gilding and paint. This would have nested inside a sarcophagus, a huge stone chest of granite. Now she was alone, with nothing between herself and a very greedy world except Emlyn.

Emlyn, whose plan had been to do bad things.

Emlyn, whose integrity did not exist.

Emlyn, the sole possessor of gold and ancient treasure.

Emlyn paced around the apartment.

It was too bad that her brothers would never know about this. Once they stopped laughing (my sister stole a mummy!), they'd be right there with the saw. Little boys love blood and gore, even when it's been dry for three thousand years.

On her next pass through the front room she saw the car keys, motionless on the high narrow table exactly as she had left them in the middle of the night. Neither parent had driven to work. She should have known that, because taking the car depended on the weather. Rain meant car. Sun meant bus or walking. She had run down sunny streets to collect the mummy from Maris's.

The car was available.

Emlyn's skin changed texture, pricking and trembling. Had it felt like this for Amaral-Re when they started to embalm her, when the natron was poured over her and the salt began its terrible work? She didn't feel a thing, Emlyn told herself sharply. She was dead.

Between mail-order catalogs nobody had had time to leaf through and the catalogs in which her brothers had circled things they couldn't live without lay the morning paper. Emlyn rarely glanced at the newspaper. News was so remote. It had no connection to the world of school and sports, of friends and fights, of triumph and hope.

A shaft of yellow sunlight cast a long, slanting rectangle over the headlines of the front page.

MUSEUM DIRECTOR ARRESTED FOR MUMMY THEFT.

She sat at the table like a grown-up, her morning paper in one hand, her glass of orange juice in the other.

Over the summer, said the article, scientists doing studies of mummies held by museums asked Dr. Brisband to let them take Amaral-Re to the hospital for X rays and CAT scans. There, radiologists could determine many things about the living person who had become that mummy — health, diseases, condition of teeth, the method by which the person had been preserved. They could determine age at death, and by charting the ages of all mummies in the study would know more about the life expectancy of people in ancient Egypt. Other scientists would take DNA samples, so the mummy's genealogy could be studied. They would try to link this supposed princess, Amaral-Re, to other royal mummies.

The scientists were reassuring. Nobody would touch the mummy during these examinations, since if afflicted by bacteria, the mummy could still rot, even after all these centuries. Moving the mummy would be done by six people, three on a side, as gently as if it were a child with a fractured back, because it was easy to fracture the dried bones.

But Dr. Brisband (said the board) cared nothing about scientific advance. Dr. Brisband was not impressed with the Egyptologists who had contacted him. He felt they did not fully respect the integrity of the mummy. Their real reason for X-raying the mummies was to see what kind of jewels covered the corpses. He believed their goal was to be in a television special, the kind that exaggerated, or even lied, about the real history and value of an object. Dr. Brisband refused to permit Amaral-Re to be included in the study.

The Board of Trustees was furious. They overruled him. By unanimous vote, they agreed to submit their mummy to such an inspection.

It took only a Monday on which the museum was closed to visitors, and when the work was done the mummy was safely returned and nobody was the wiser.

And then the board was shown the X rays of the mummy.

Stupifying X rays; mesmerizing X rays.

The newspaper quoted a trustee. "Clearly, our mummy was a treasure lode. We instructed Dr. Brisband to arrange to have the mummy unwrapped. The museum is in need of funds. We have so many projects on which we cannot begin. What if we could pay for our new direction and our expanding collection by retrieving the treasures inside the mummy?"

The board had voted to unwrap the mummy? thought Emlyn. *The board?* The people responsible? The people voted into place to protect the museum? They, like Donovan, like Lovell and Maris and Jack, they, too, just wanted gold?

"It was my idea," the chairman said, "to have a party. This idea met with great excitement. How much would you pay in order to take your turn unwrapping a mummy? I'll tell you what you'd pay. A lot. You would get to be one of the first people on earth to see that gold. Think what a major fund-raiser the party would be! People would come from all over the world."

No doubt this was true. People who had taken trips to the Cairo Museum, stared up at the Great Pyramid, shivered in awe at the feet of the Sphinx — of course, they would pay a fortune to be present at the unveiling of an ancient Egyptian treasure. They might not even care whether it turned out to be gold. They would just want to be there.

Emlyn was shivering all over.

Amaral, lying on her back, huge dark eyes staring at yet another ceiling, while people gnawed on her ribs like dogs. I'll have a leg, I'll have a wrist, give me a bone, give me a jewel.

Television cameras and silver-haired commentators, paid Egyptologists and snickering board members. Let's auction her off! What am I bid? First the bones and then the skull.

Dr. Brisband had referred to this at his Friends' meeting, but Emlyn had been too excited about her own project to listen. Emlyn had been scornful of Lovell, who had not even listened to herself. But Emlyn was no better; Emlyn had paid no attention to anything that mattered.

According to the paper, Dr. Brisband had had a serious fight with his Board of Trustees. The museum mummy party was to take place in January. Dr. Brisband said they would damage the mummy over his dead body! He would call in museum experts from all over the world; he would show them. But they overruled him once more and set the date for the mummy unwrapping party.

And now the mummy had been stolen. What more likely person to have snatched that mummy from its bier than Dr. Brisband himself?

"Dr. Brisband," said the chairman, "would like us to believe that somebody managed to get into the museum — in spite of guards — and spirit the mummy away. That's ridiculous. He stole the mummy for himself. He knows its value. The trustees have obtained a search warrant for Dr. Brisband's home."

The police confirmed that Dr. Harris Brisband had been alone in the museum when the mummy was taken. The guests at that private party had been in the theater, had come and gone by theater doors, and had not had access to the museum.

The man Bob, thought Emlyn, must have been a board member on Dr. Brisband's side. He could say he'd seen Dr. Brisband briefly on the night the mummy was taken, but Dr. Brisband had stayed on alone.

They can't arrest him just because he was in the museum, thought Emlyn. He's the director, he's always in the museum, there's every reason why he ought to be in the museum and not a single reason why it's suspicious. They don't have any evidence because they can't have any evidence, because I am the only person on earth who knows exactly what happened.

She began to laugh a high, shuddery laugh. It was not loud and it was not strong, but it convulsed her, and she shivered at the horrible sound of her own laugh.

She could not return the mummy to the museum. The trustees would snatch Amaral-Re from her arms and send out the invitations for the unwrapping party.

She could not return the mummy to Dr. Brisband. He was safe only if he did *not* have the mummy. Were she to put the mummy on his doorstep, he would really be arrested.

If she tried to protect Dr. Brisband by saying, "I did it," not only would *she* be arrested (if they'd arrest the director of the city museum, they would certainly arrest a plain old high school senior), but they would insist that she produce the mummy.

And then the same thing would happen: The trustees would arrange for Amaral-Re, princess, to be destroyed.

She had said to Lovell and Donovan, to Maris and Jack, that pyramids were beginning to look logical.

Indeed.

For where — where on this earth? — was she going to hide a mummy, if even the museum wanted to destroy that mummy?

Emlyn went back into her bedroom. She held her hand at a slant in front of her face so she would not have to see Amaral-Re's sad eyes focused on her ceiling. But it was impossible. She knelt by her own bed, as one saying prayers, and stared at the gold and the indigo-blue of the guest in her house.

You are wrong, Harris Brisband, thought Emlyn. Amaral is not an object. She is herself. I owe you, Amaral. I became yours when I took you. And you became mine.

The integrity of the mummy.

Integrity meant having honor and truth in your soul. But it also meant completeness, soundness, unbroken perfection.

Emlyn lacked integrity. She had stolen.

But for the moment, Amaral still possessed her integrity.

Emlyn took her museum card from its hiding place in an old shoe box filled with index cards, notes from projects beginning in third grade. Yes, she was right. That card, too, used the word *stolen*.

My heart has stolen forth and goes quietly to a place it knows well.

Was Amaral talking about death or love? Had she stolen away from her house to meet a boy she adored? Or had she stolen her last breath and gone quietly to another world?

And me, thought Emlyn. What have I prepared for all my life? To let Dr. Brisband be accused of stealing from his own museum? To let an innocent man lose his career and his future?

But if I tell, I will have to produce the mummy. And then it won't be Lovell and Jack and Maris and Donovan with the rusty saw on the kitchen table. It will be the Board of Trustees with a shining stainless steel saw on the gleaming expanse of their table at their fund-raiser.

And Amaral's integrity, and mine, will be ruined forever.

Eighteen

Emlyn took every book, CD, stuffed animal, per-
fume bottle, and piece of junk off one of her
shelves. She lifted the board from its angle irons.
She slid Amaral onto the board, which was
exactly long enough but not nearly wide enough.
The board was twelve inches wide. Amaral, at
the shoulders, was several inches more.

From a long, shallow kitchen drawer filled with
oddities, Emlyn got a roll of wrapping paper. It
took an entire roll of Scotch tape and every
scrap of wrapping paper in the house: birthday,
Christmas, Valentine's Day, and wedding shower
included. Amaral looked spectacular. Anybody
would want that present.

Emlyn put on a jacket with huge baggy pockets. Then she grabbed a flat sheet from the linen
closet, folded it until she could jam it into one of

the pockets, dropped the car keys into another pocket, and shouldered Amaral: board, paper, ribbons, mummy, and all.

"Wow," said the elevator guy. "Somebody's getting a cool present."

"You bet," said Emlyn. "I don't do things by halves."

He went with her to the car, and together they opened the rear of the wagon, and Emlyn crawled inside to put the backseat down. Now she took the foot end of Amaral and the elevator guy helped with the head end, and they slid the mummy neatly into the Ford. "Thanks," said Emlyn.

"What is it?" he asked.

"That papier-mâché doll I brought in earlier this morning," she said. "It's a surprise."

"Way cool," he said. "I want somebody to spend that much time and energy on me."

Time and energy had certainly been spent on the dead girl three thousand years ago. Sixty days of embalming. The funeral and procession. The love and sorrow that must have surrounded her; the song and dance and funeral feast.

Emlyn covered the mummy with the bedsheet. Her mother wasn't a buyer of plain white sheets. She liked sheets with flowers or cowboys, with plaids or snowmen. Their linen closet was a history of childhood taste in sheets. This sheet was from when her brothers were in love with choo-choo trains.

Now the shape in the station wagon was neither a mummy nor a gift-wrapped present. It was just a mess: wrinkled, swollen laundry.

Where, thought Emlyn, is a place that's dry and dark and hidden and has a room for a five-foot stiff?

Stiff, she thought. Rhymes with skiff. Sounds like scull.

She and Amaral drove out of the parking level and into the street. Although it was not the direct route, something made her take the road past the museum.

She couldn't even get close. The block was thronged with people. This was the crowd museums always hoped to attract and seldom did.

From a block away she could see people high on the museum steps with microphones and cameras. Across the street, parked in the middle of everything as if to thumb its nose at people who used parking spaces and put quarters in, was the network van.

A traffic policeman was yanking his arm in the air as if he were hauling on some heavy pulley. He wanted Emlyn out of that intersection. She rolled her window down and pulled up next to him and said, "What is happening at the museum?"

"A press conference," said the policeman. "There's nothing like a mummy-stealing to bring out the crowds. I need you to drive on, please."

He did not look inside the Ford. He did not really even look at Emlyn. He was looking at the big picture and missing all the little pieces.

She parked four blocks away. After locking the doors, she actually circled the car, trying the handles. This was not a good day for some hophead in need of a radio to look under the choo-choo sheet instead.

She jogged down the road, joining the crowd and pressing rudely through. Finally, she reached the bottom step of the museum entrance where the cameras and reporters and police stood.

Police. Now that she was out of her car, no heavy, solid, locked doors between herself and them, she was afraid. They were no friendly neighborhood helpers, the ones they told you about in kindergarten. These were men and women eager to slam you to the ground, handcuff you, and arrest you for mummy theft.

They'd be very polite, she said to herself. They'd say, "Ma'am? Would you be willing to discuss this with us?"

They were hung with weaponry, as the mummy had been hung with jewels: arms held slightly away from their own sides, ready to pounce.

On me, thought Emlyn.

She felt sick and afraid, guilty and visible.

The crowds shifted and changed around her. She had not eaten in a long time. She hoped she wouldn't faint or do any other stupid thing to call attention to herself.

The criminal, she remembered, returns to the scene of his crime.

It was true. She had.

It seemed that Dr. Brisband was not locked up, because he and several others stood around on the very top step, waiting for the microphones to be readied.

Now that she thought of it, they wouldn't waste jail space on him. This was like computer theft or Wall Street theft. White-collar stuff, where you said, "Naughty, naughty" and made them pay a fine, and then they could write a book about it and go on talk shows.

A very attractive woman a little older than Emlyn's parents was the first to speak. Her frosted hair was shoulder length, blunt cut; her fine suit showed off slender legs and trim ankles. Heavy designer jewelry made clear her excellent and expensive taste. She introduced herself as the chairman of the Board of Trustees.

She went over the same things that Emlyn had read in the paper, making Dr. Brisband sound like a snake. "We hope," she said as frostily as her hair, "that Harris Brisband will behave honorably and return the mummy to the museum."

The crowd murmured, but Emlyn could not tell what they were thinking. Were they thinking of gold and what it was worth? Or were they thinking of the mummy they had loved as children and brought their children to see, too?

The moment the questions began, it was all too clear where the interests of the crowd lay.

"Once he gives the mummy back, can the public buy tickets to this party?"

"How much will they cost?"

"Does everybody get to do some unwrapping?"

"Are you going to auction the mummy's gold off or display it in the museum?"

"Do you just get to keep the gold, or can you have a piece of the mummy?"

"On a talk show last night, I don't know if you saw it, but they were saying that powdered mummy was very well known centuries ago as a cancer treatment."

"Did the board plan this whole thing as a publicity stunt so you can get lots more money for the mummy bones?"

Nobody answered. The chairman just stood there, being graceful. Eventually, giving the chairman the kind of look Emlyn wanted to develop and give stupid people, Dr. Harris Brisband took the mike.

"From time immemorial, people have wanted to destroy mummies. There is something about their hidden bodies that entrances us. The desire to be vandals is common to many of us. We want to slice and destroy. To rip and tear.

"A mummy cannot be unwrapped. Every bandage is glued to the one below. The only way to get down to the bones is with a saw. That was explained to the board. They cannot get what they perceive to be jewelry without destroying the mummy. They don't care. As far as they are concerned, the mummy is nothing. It does not deserve to exist. They are eager to hack the mummy to bits. They are motivated by greed. They want to sell tickets; they want to be on television.

"This mummy has been displayed in our museum for nearly one hundred years. By reason of the will of the original founder and donor of the museum, the mummy is for the children. She is to be on exhibit at all times, at their eye level. If the trustees continue with their heinous plans, they are breaking the trust they were given."

189

I was one of those children, thought Emlyn.

The board would fire Dr. Brisband. He would never find another job as museum director. His future had been torn away, just as Amaral's linen would be torn if those trustees got hold of her.

"When are you going to return the mummy?" demanded a reporter.

"I do not possess the mummy."

"Who does possess the mummy?"

"I have no idea. The police have no clues."

The police have no clues, thought Emlyn. Relief washed over her like cool rain.

The police had no clues.

"I hoped it was a Mischief Night or Halloween prank," said Dr. Brisband, "and if so, we would find the mummy on our doorstep the first of November. But you reporters and this foolish board have ruined that hope. Now, because of you, whoever has the mummy will destroy it, hoping for gold. I cannot stress enough that the value of the mummy is in the mummy itself. Her antiquity, her beauty, her integrity."

But the reporters had lost interest. They were on their cell phones, getting instructions for other stories, yanking up their cables, slouching back to their van. The chairman and Dr. Brisband were merely tape, to be used if there was airtime and cut if there was not.

The crowd dwindled. A few went into the museum but most drifted off. It turned out they were just office workers from nearby buildings, sitting on the steps in the sun for lunch. Dr. Brisband and the other museum officials went inside.

Emlyn leaned against the heavy stone balustrade of the great museum steps. Every town and city had its cemeteries. All religions wanted their dead to lie in safety, and in groups, and with markers. Nobody wanted her grandmother shoveled up and auctioned, her wedding ring ripped off her finger.

But if that grandmother had died three thousand years ago? When did a body stop being sacred — and start being funny? When did a person stop being honored and start being a party game? Was there a cutoff date? If Amaral had died twenty years ago, they would still be careful with her. But a hundred years? Two hundred?

Perhaps you stopped being a dead person and became *stuff* once your grandchildren and your great grandchildren were dead, too. Then your whole family was just stuff, and it was fine for strangers to rip your ring off your finger.

A chilly finger stroked the back of Emlyn's neck. A hot breath followed.

Emlyn leaped away as if from bee stings.

"Emlyn, Emlyn," said Maris. She was smiling. "There isn't anybody who can slip into a trance the way you can," said Maris. "We've been standing behind you for fifteen minutes. Your little face mirrored a thousand emotions, Emlyn."

Donovan was smiling, too. "You never thought of glancing behind you, Emlyn. That's step one, you know. Keep track of the enemy."

Lovell was not smiling.

Jack was not smiling.

"Cute trick with my mother," said Maris.

Emlyn felt as if there were dozens of them. They, too, held their arms a little out from their

191

sides as if they, too, were armed with revolvers and clubs, ready to pounce. They were, after all, an excellent team.

"We're going to follow you," said Maris politely. "There are four of us. We will work in shifts. You won't go anywhere without us. We'll find the mummy."

Emlyn said nothing. It seemed pointless to show up for the last two periods of school, but she couldn't go back to the car now. She walked slowly. Donovan walked on her left. Maris on her right. Jack and Lovell paired up behind her.

"I wish that dumb mummy had never been taken from Egypt," said Jack. "We hate you, you hate us. And the thing is, this was supposed to be so much fun."

"I'm having fun," said Donovan. "You were right about one thing. This is better than cows. Now the point is, Emlyn, we're going to get that gold. You know it's worth it if the whole board voted to do the same thing. There is no place for you to stick that mummy, Emlyn, except your own apartment. So, Emmy, don't worry about Maris's cute little idea of us tailing you all over the city. We're all five of us going to your house."

Good, thought Emlyn. Because the mummy isn't there, and there's no sign that it ever was there. Of course, if we waste time going to my house, what do I do about hiding the mummy and getting the car back for my parents?

"Come on, Em, lighten up," said Maris. "We're friends. We want to do this together."

"What about Dr. Brisband?" asked Emlyn.

"He can take care of himself," said Lovell. "He's that kind of guy. Come on, Emlyn. Where's the mummy?"

The car keys felt heavy and hidden in her jacket pocket. She did not let her hand stray over them. She reached into her pants pocket and took out her house key instead. She handed it to Maris. "You guys go have a fun time with the mummy. I'm going to school. I can't miss calculus. If I miss even one class, I can't figure out what I'm doing. I'm going to be an engineer, you know, and I need advanced math." She was not taking calculus. She did not have a math course this semester. But she was fond of fibbing. "Feel free to split up," suggested Emlyn. "Some of you may tail me. Others may enter my bedroom and look under the mattress."

Maris took the key uncertainly.

"You have lots of time," said Emlyn. "My brothers have sports after school, and my parents are never home before six. The knives are in a drawer to the left of the sink in case you actually do find a mummy and wish to slice it open."

Emlyn bet that though they were willing to break into a museum or watch Emlyn do it, and they were willing to rip apart a priceless mummy, and they had been willing to enter an unused summer cottage, they were not quite willing to go into somebody else's house, even with the key, and poke around and open drawers. She crossed the street when the walk light came on and turned toward the high school. It was not a short walk. They had many blocks to go. They were all, except Donovan, athletes, and when Emlyn started to run, they all, except Donovan, ran with her.

"This is a bluff," said Maris, looking at the key. "The mummy *is* in your room. You don't have any other place to put it."

"I agree," said Lovell. "Let Emlyn go to school. We'll hit the apartment. It's not breaking and entering; she gave her good dear friends her key."

"Slow down," said Jack. "Wait for Donovan to catch up."

Emlyn did not slow down.

Jack said, "I don't think the mummy is at her place. I think she took it somewhere else."

"Like where?" demanded Maris. "She takes it out of my bedroom, by sheer accident I call home to ask my mother about something else and find out, and only half an hour later we find her at the museum. She didn't have time to go anyplace but home."

"I had time," said Emlyn, "to go to the museum."

Lovell grabbed her arm and yanked her to a stop. "What are you talking about?" said Lovell.

Emlyn wasn't up for a street scene, so she stood still, letting Lovell tighten her fingers as hard as she wanted. "I took the mummy back," said Emlyn. "I have a master key, remember? I can get in and out whenever I want."

Jack was stunned. *"You put the mummy back in the museum?"*

Maris began laughing, in a sort of stunned admiration. "You *did* put it back, didn't you? I love that. It's amazing and insane. Who do you think you are, the Robin Hood of mummies? Steal and give back?"

"No, she didn't," said Lovell. "She doesn't want the integrity of the mummy compromised. That means she can't let the museum board have it, either. They'll compromise the integrity even more than we will. They'll make a fortune while they're sawing it open."

And then Emlyn made a mistake. She talked too much. "I put it in the basement where there are hundreds of crates and piles and shelves. It's just another thing under a canvas. They'll never find it, you see. It will be safe, but they won't know."

Maris narrowed her eyes. "If that were true, you wouldn't say so, Emlyn. All we have to do is call the trustees and they'd go get the mummy. You wouldn't have preserved its integrity after all. So you're lying. You made up getting into the museum basement."

Donovan caught up.

"The big question," he said, "isn't what she makes up. It's how fast she moves. She absolutely did not have enough time to get from one apartment to another and then to the museum on foot. *She drove.* So who knows what kind of car she drives? Because it's parked out there. And it's carrying a mummy."

Nineteen

"I wanted risk," Emlyn told them, walking toward school. They walked with her. They didn't know what else to do. None of them knew what her family car looked like or whether Donovan's guess was correct. Bluff, thought Emlyn. You can do this.

"I could have taken up ice climbing, I suppose," she said in a quiet, friendly voice, as if they were buddies sitting over Cokes and hamburgers. "Or piloting small planes or studying live volcanoes. I could have gotten a sea kayak and explored caves. But I took up theft. I wanted to take something that wasn't mine. And I've done it. And it was incredibly exciting. But I thought it would be like a skit on a stage, just one little act. No. It was bigger and more wrong than I thought it would be."

They kept pace with her, but they were staring down at the sidewalk.

"We aren't criminals," said Emlyn. "You're not going to kick in the window of my car and jump-start it, Donovan. You're not going to shove me against that building and rip the car keys out of my pocket, Jack. You're not going to pull my hair and kick me, Lovell. And Maris isn't going to break into my house." She held out her hand for the key, and Maris, embarrassed, dropped it into her palm. I am the better actress after all, thought Emlyn. "We took a precious object," she said, "and at this moment, yes, she is in my hands. And it turns out she is a trust. I am her trustee. I have to do the right thing."

They were almost at the school.

Had they fallen for this? Did they feel uncomfortable and uncertain, the way she wanted them to?

Jack actually held the front door of the school open for the others. Maris and Lovell entered first, and after a long, uncertain look at Emlyn, they went their separate ways down the halls, shrugging off the event, moving on with life.

Emlyn came in next and then Donovan, and Jack said, "Let us know, Emmy," and she nodded and looked at her watch to see which class she ought to be in.

Jack hurried to catch up to Maris, but Donovan walked alongside Emlyn. "You don't have calculus," he said in his nicest voice. "I'm in calculus, see. I know everybody taking the course. And I don't believe for one minute that you're going to give that mummy back to that museum.

197

You loved stealing that mummy. You're like me. You hide everything you can. But I'm like you, so I see through it. You're keeping that gold for yourself, Emlyn. Well, forget it. I'm hanging on. You're not going to dump me. I'm getting gold, too. It's a lottery, see, and I have a ticket, and you're not taking it away from me."

Emlyn nodded. She thought, This was the person I thought I might fall for. I was wrong at every turn. I was wrong about me, wrong about them, wrong about stealing, wrong about fun, wrong about my brilliance.

She said, "Well, come on in, then, and share my table in physics." She walked into physics. Donovan took an uncertain step into the door. Emlyn did not look back but walked through the large classroom in spite of the lecture going on and into the laboratory shared with the chemistry class next door. She threaded her way through people obeying the steps in their lab books. The laboratory was in the corner and had two exits. Emlyn went out the other way, into the other hall, where Donovan could not see her. In two quick steps she was in another stairwell, racing down, gong out another door, and running to the far corner for another taxi.

She used her key.

It was dark inside and damp. She worried a little about the damp. But it wouldn't be for long. She shifted some of the other objects lying crosswise over the beams and yanked out an old tarp. She wrapped the huge, shining birthday present in the tarp and set it in the very back, stacking old broken oars and some out-of-date flotation devices on top of it.

The boathouse was in constant use. But Emlyn had participated in this sport for three years. People were single-minded. They did not explore dark corners. They did not wonder what was in the back, and they did not care what was discarded.

She put her hand on the bulge that was Amaral-Re's head and whispered, "I'll be back."

She locked the boathouse, went back to the Ford, drove home, and smiled at Donovan, who was pacing on the sidewalk in front of her building. "Come on up," she said. "I owe you a pizza."

But I do not owe you a mummy.

Emlyn's friends were tickled at the extent of the crush Donovan had on her. How adorable it was; he was like a puppy, following her. They loved it.

But he was not like a puppy. He was like a pit bull. He had his teeth in this, and he was not letting go. Whenever he stood near her, she felt the intensity of his desire. Not for her; she was meaningless. For gold. She could imagine him in some California gold rush, standing by some icy mountain stream, ready to knife the man who got there first.

She rarely saw Lovell or Maris or Jack, and that was natural. She had rarely seen them before their senior prank plans. But Donovan was everywhere, with a copy of her schedule he had convinced the office secretary to give him.

It took her three days to slip away from Donovan.

By then, other seniors had gotten hold of a huge advertising balloon from a car dealership and tied its ropes to the steel beam in the bell tower, and senior prank was over and done with. The dealership didn't mind. Advertising is advertising.

On Halloween, Emlyn took her brothers and their friends door-to-door in their building, gathering candy and gum and paperback books and apples. Lots of kids were mummies.

The day after Halloween, Emlyn made it to the public library without being followed. She waited patiently at various corners. No Donovan appeared. No Lovell, Maris, or Jack.

She waited another twenty minutes for the particular computer she wanted. It was the only one whose screen was entirely sheltered from passersby, and the only one facing the door. She got on the Internet, ready to shut down quickly. If she left the screen on, the next person could follow her trail and see where she had been. If the next person was Donovan, he was smart enough to figure out her plans.

She read a few sentences, scrolled a few lines, checked the door and the people coming and going, and read again. Truly the Internet was astonishing. So many sites. She began to have hope. There was a way out.

She was standing in the fiction section in front of New Mysteries when Donovan caught up to her. Emlyn did not actually like made-up stories; she liked real history, science, and biography.

But she pulled one off the shelf at random and smiled at Donovan. He didn't smile back. She thought that if they had not been in a public place he would have grabbed her and tried to shake out of her the location of the mummy. For the first time, she was physically afraid of him.

They were not criminals. They were not bad people. But if you wanted something badly enough you might take a very bad step to get it. Not only did Emlyn have to get the mummy to safety, she had to accomplish this publicly so Donovan would know that the mummy was beyond his reach forever.

She took a bus home, which she rarely did. She wanted the company of all those strangers. She did not want the company of Donovan. She had it anyway. At least he could not come in the apartment with her.

At home, she called the store where he used to work before he started following her. "Hi," she said to the manager, giving him Maris's name. "We're planning a surprise party for Donovan, and we need to know when he's at work so he doesn't catch on to any of the preparations."

The manager, who thought this touching and sweet, the sort of thing teenagers had done in the good old days, immediately gave her Donovan's schedule. "He took this week off," explained the manager. "He had to study for exams. But he goes back to his regular schedule on Thursday."

There were no exams the week after Halloween, but it sounded good.

So on Thursday , knowing Donovan was safely stocking shelves, Emlyn went to a huge, busy chain store, a print and copy shop where you could also rent computer time.

She had written out the e-mail in her room, getting every sentence exactly right. Then she ripped her practice e-mail in shreds and came here without it. Typed onto the screen, it looked as suspect as a message from the kind of psychopath who stalked celebrities.

I wish to open negotiations for the protection of a mummy I now possess.

Right. How quickly would *that* message go into the trash?

She worked and reworked her sentences. No matter what she wrote, it read back badly. Nobody would bother with her nonsense. Her brainstorm was no longer shot full of brilliance. It was a pathetic attempt at sidelining her theft.

She was out of time for this afternoon. Life and its annoying schedules — in this case, taking one of her brothers to the orthodontist — got in the way. Emlyn sent the e-mail.

All through the orthodontist appointment (which included fifteen minutes of waiting in the magazine room and fifteen more waiting in the chair), Emlyn catalogued her stupidity. If this didn't work, she had no more ideas. None.

Friday, Donovan was due at work at two thirty, meaning that he had to leave school the instant the bell rang. At two forty-five, Emlyn went to one of the ranks of pay phones in the school lobby. They were not booths but slanted, open cubes. There was no privacy, and yet nobody paid any attention, so she felt relatively safe. She couldn't use her phone card, she didn't want the bill to arrive and her parents to ask about the numbers. So she had enough quarters to call New York.

When the phone was answered, a flush of humiliation burned Emlyn's cheeks. She had never felt so wholly stupid. "I'm the one who e-mailed about the mummy," she said. It was just a receptionist. She would have to explain it all to some clerk, some secretary, and get slowly passed from person to person, endlessly repeating her nonsense.

"Yes, of course," said the receptionist. "We were waiting for your call. Let me transfer you."

Emlyn felt substance beside her. Bulk. Shadow. She whirled. It was Jack, smiling. Maris behind him. Emlyn felt a sob rising in her throat. It was too much. It was not fair! She had thought the rest had thrown in the towel, given up.

"I have to go," said Emlyn. "There are people here."

"Don't hang up!" said the person on the other end. The man there sounded breathless and frantic, which was a good sign; a yes-we're-interested-in-a-missing-mummy sign.

" 'Bye," said Emlyn politely. "Talk to you later." She disconnected. She smiled at Jack and Maris, dropped more change into the phone, and dialed again. It was just random numbers, she didn't care who answered or what they said. She just wanted to hang onto the receiver instead of deal with Jack and Maris.

"Who were you calling?" said Maris. "Police? FBI? Museum moguls around the world? Distant cousins who own empty tombs?"

"All of the above," said Emlyn. "But my cousin with the empty tomb doesn't want a mummy, so I'm back to square one."

It took the rest of the weekend to make her calls, but Donovan worked weekends, and Maris and Jack and Lovell had a thousand better things to do than wander around hoping to catch Emlyn on the phone or shifting museum treasures.

The final arrangements were actually quite easy to make. They never asked her name, they never demanded details, they just agreed. "Why us?" they said during one conversation.

"Who else is there?" she said, and they had to agree.

She arranged things for Tuesday at four P.M., when Donovan was at work and the others had after-school activities. It was a viciously cold and grim November day. No Egyptian princess had ever felt weather like this. Emlyn hated to think of Amaral-Re, frozen and stiff in her box in the boathouse.

She left school, looking carefully and seeing nobody. She paused as usual at various corners and inside the sheltered, invisible openings of stores, but nobody followed her. She began the long hike to the river.

The river was hard to find, for over the decades it had been shut away by raised highways and embankments. There was only one point at which there was a park, and Emlyn, wishing she had a scarf and mittens, walked in bitter wind to one of the benches that lined a strip of grass near the boat launch. The grass was brown and crunchy, and the bench was so cold to sit on she almost stood up again. But this was where they expected to find her. This river, this park, this bench.

There were no pleasure boats still in the water by November and very few still in their berths at the marinas. River traffic for the winter would be a few tugs and barges and the occasional sight-seeing boat for spotting eagles. This afternoon the river was gray and silent, a cold reflection of a cold sky.

Other people had come to gaze at the river, but they wisely came in cars whose heaters they kept running and whose radios were probably playing. They seemed to drive in, reassure them-selves that the river was still there, and drive back out.

Emlyn sat for quite a while, getting colder and colder.

They were late. Or they were not coming. Or had they decided on some other ending for her?

Her heart began to hurt a little, and then her stomach, and then her head. What was she wait-ing for now? What had the fates planned that she had not been able to plan for herself?

Donovan sat down next to her. He was smiling. "I just wanted you to know, Emlyn. You're not the smartest page in the book. Or as we say in boat lingo, you're rowing with one oar."

She couldn't speak.

He held up a key.

It matched the key in her palm.

"You stood outside the school looking left and

looking right and peeking here and peering there," said Donovan, grinning, "and I thought, This is it. She's on her way. You are so pathetic, really you are, Emlyn. You were looking all over the place for somebody on foot. You never checked out the cars. It was a picnic to follow you in my car. Once I realized where you were going — and I have to say I kicked myself; I should have thought of the boathouse — I drove back to get the key from the athletic office."

Emlyn stared down the river at the cold gray water and wished she could see around the bend. But life never let you see around the bend. "I thought you were supposed to be at work."

"I am. But even the best employee lets the company down now and then, you know. And who cares about a little after-school job, anyway? In an hour, I'm going to have gold, not minimum wage." He got up off the bench and walked toward the boathouse.

I lost, thought Emlyn. I cannot fight him. It's just what I said to Maris: I'm back at square one. If I hit him or kick him, we'll have a fragile mummy in the way.

She had not thought of the boat launch as being isolated because, of course, when she had crew, this was a very busy place. But now, the afternoon already drawing to a wintry, dark close, there were few cars, no pay phone, nobody on the river, and the only traffic was high above, screaming past at seventy miles an hour, never even seeing the river, let alone Emlyn.

She went after him, thinking, I do have to call

the police, then. I decided to throw in my lot with Amaral-Re, and if I can't save myself at the same time, then I can't. Of course, now that I'm ready to give up, I have no phone.

She considered tapping on the drivers' windows of the river-watchers' cars, saying, "Do you have a phone? I need to call 911."

Close to the boathouse was a four-door Mercedes. Its plates said MUSEUM. Emlyn had not noticed it, just as she had noticed so little in all her skulking around. The driver's door opened, the driver got out, and Dr. Brisband stepped in front of Donovan. "This," he said politely, "would be an awkward time to get involved, young man."

Donovan recognized Dr. Brisband. He paused, uncertain.

How can he be here? thought Emlyn, aghast. I didn't get in touch with him.

"Good afternoon, young lady," said Dr. Brisband to Emlyn. "I remember you from the interview we did not have."

She was going to start crying. She had held together through every mistake, large and small, and now she was going to cry like a baby. "It was supposed to be a high school prank, Dr. Brisband. But it got serious."

"I think it was serious for you from the beginning. And I hope you realize how serious the consequences are."

Her tears flowed over. "I'm not crying because of what might happen to me," she told him. "I'm ready for any of that. And I apologize for the

207

position I put you in. It's just that I really thought I could make it turn out okay after all. I really thought I could rescue Amaral-Re."

"Indeed," said Dr. Brisband, "I believe you have." He pointed downriver. A large white power yacht with a high prow and several decks was sliding toward them at considerable speed. It had grace and style. It had no name.

"What's going on?" said Donovan.

"When she realized there was no way to keep the mummy safe," said Dr. Brisband, "your friend e-mailed the Egyptian Embassy in New York and began negotiations. She asked if they would keep the mummy and also assist our museum factions coming to a decision about the mummy's fate."

Donovan sighed. Then he shrugged. Then he said, "You win, Emmy."

The boat pulled up against the pilings of the dock, protected from scratches by its heavy white rubber circles. Emlyn caught a rope and tied it, and a crew member jumped off and tied the other rope. The powerful engine continued to throb. They didn't plan to stay long. Two men and two women got off. They shook hands with Dr. Brisband.

They looked at Emlyn, but they did not shake hands.

I got what I asked for, she thought. I did something bad, and they know it, and they accept where we are now, and they're going to pick up the pieces. But that doesn't make me a good guy who deserves an introduction and a handshake. I did not win.

She unlocked the boathouse and pointed to the tarp.

Donovan came in, too.

In utter silence, the package was lowered. The tarp removed.

"Why gift-wrapping paper?" asked Dr. Brisband.

She was embarrassed. "I had to protect her. I couldn't stand to see her in trash bags anymore." She gestured at Donovan. "It made the others see her as trash."

Dr. Brisband slowly removed the wrapping paper.

In the unlit damp, surrounded by slender sculls as mysterious in the shadows as any pyramid artifact, a party of seven looked down at Amaral-Re, and she looked back at them, as she always had, silent and elegant and eternal.

When the boat was gone and the mummy had disappeared around the bend in the river, safe in the hands of her descendants, Donovan offered Emlyn a ride home, which she refused, and Dr. Brisband offered her a ride home, which she accepted.

He said, "The only oddity that took place the week before the mummy theft was the unfinished interview by the girl reporter. There was nobody by that name attending any school in the city. And when somebody claiming to possess the mummy got in touch with the Egyptian Embassy, I, of course, was notified. This girl was requesting a meeting in the city schools' boathouse? It took only a moment with last year's yearbook to find photographs of the crew teams. My secretary and I recognized you immediately."

He was taking the right turns. He knew where she lived. He'll come inside, she thought. He'll tell my parents. Of course, he will, he'll have to.

Dr. Brisband said, "So what was this about?"

"We were going to hang the mummy from the bell tower for Mischief Night," she said. "I didn't realize how real she would be. I didn't realize, once I had her in my hands, that I had to do my part in keeping her for the next generation to dream of ancient Egypt. I began to see we couldn't hang her at all. She would fall apart from being thrown around. Then we found out about the gold. The others wanted her gold. They wanted the very same party the trustees wanted. I was the thief, and I was wrong, but at least it turned out that I don't have greed. I just wanted to pull it off. But once I pulled it off — I had her. She was my responsibility." Emlyn mopped up her tears. "What will happen to you? Are you fired? Are you arrested? Is your career ruined? Was it wrong to call the Egyptian Embassy?"

He did not turn toward her street after all. She wondered if she should correct him. Or was he heading for the police station?

It was dark. People were bent over in the wind, clutching their coats, scurrying toward warmth. Emlyn was cold from fear.

"The board was upset to find themselves the focus of negative press," said Dr. Brisband. "The museum world attacked them. You must not

210

believe everything you see on television or read in the papers. I was not arrested, just threatened with it. However, I probably would have not been able to save the mummy. The board was far too pleased with their party and their auction. As for my future, we will wait for the Egyptians to announce the arrival of the mummy in their hands. It's a difficult precedent you are setting. It implies the museum does not have the right to decide what becomes of its own exhibits. But under the circumstances, you did well by Amaral-Re, although you did not do well by the museum or by me."

She could not figure out where they were going. She stopped looking at the signs on the corners. Wherever he was headed, they would get there, and something would happen, and it would not be in her control.

"Are you going to tell your parents?" he asked.

"Not if I don't have to. I want them to think I'm a good person."

"I'm not sure what I think. You are a person who only half wants to be good, Emlyn. The choice is yours. I hope you don't go wrong. If you go right, you might aim for curator. The curator, you know, is the guardian. The one who cares."

He touched an automatic garage opener on his visor, and Emlyn stared in astonishment as heavy doors opened and he drove into the courtyard of the museum. Was she going to have to face the board or something?

"Just curiosity," he said, smiling. "I want you to

211

show me how you did it. The public isn't here right now; we're having a touring exhibit set up. You and I can ramble."

He parked, opened his door, and headed inside. Emlyn followed. Was this it? Was it over? Was he actually taking this so easily? So lightly?

It seemed such a bargain, to be getting off. Whatever danger there had been, was it gone? Dried to a husk in the Egyptian sun?

They came into the offices and the old mansion wing.

"Oh, Dr. Brisband!" exclaimed a young man Emlyn had never seen. "Thank heaven you're here! This is a nightmare. The Texas people are furious. We neglected to — "

"I'm coming," said Dr. Brisband calmly. "Emlyn, why don't you come along? You can see how a curator spends his time."

He doesn't want to leave me alone in his office, thought Emlyn wryly.

It turned out to be an exhibit of Texas history with lots of stuff about the Alamo and President Johnson and ranching. Emlyn could hardly be bothered to look. She supposed that a museum whose mummy had been stolen was not going to snare traveling exhibits of crown jewels from England. Thanks to her, this museum would always have to settle for old saddles and barbed wire collections.

Dr. Brisband soothed the lighting people, whose feelings had been hurt by the Texans, whose feelings had been hurt by the lack of concern for proper lighting.

And then something awesome and astonishing

was lifted from its packing materials. It was a sword so gleaming, so burnished that it caught all light and blinded Emlyn with its beauty. The hilt was heavy with jewels that anyone would turn pirate to own. Swirls of engraving decorated the blade. Who could have used, in battle, so long and wide a weapon? It must have been held by a conquistador as he marched into Mexico, thrusting it skyward, thinking himself a god.

Emlyn had never seen anything so magnificent.

She yearned to stroke that shining metal, feel how sharp the blade might be, stare into the glittering facets of those jewels.

She dropped her eyes and looked at the floor so Dr. Brisband would not see what was reflected in her eyes.

My heart has stolen forth, thought Emlyn, *and goes quietly to a place it knows well.*

And what does my heart know best? And what does my heart want?

To be good?

Or to pull it off again?

About the Author

Caroline B. Cooney lives in a small seacoast village in Connecticut. She writes every day on a word processor and then goes for a long walk down the beach to figure out what she's going to write the following day. She's written over fifty books for young people, including, *The Party's Over*; the acclaimed *The Face on the Milk Carton* Trilogy; *Flight #116 Is Down*, which won the 1994 Golden Sower Award for Young Adults, the 1995 Rebecca Caudill Young Readers' Book Award, and was selected as an ALA Recommended Book for the Reluctant Young Adult Reader; *Flash Fire*; *Emergency Room*; *The Stranger*; and *Twins. Wanted* and *The Terrorist* were both 1998 ALA Quick Picks for Reluctant Young Adult Readers.

Ms. Cooney reads as much as possible, and has three grown children.